THE BLUERIDGE JUNCTION BOYS

FIGHT FOR IT

MICAH & COLE

A.D. ELLIS

WWW.FACEBOOK.COM/ADELLISAUTHOR

COPYRIGHT © 2017

COVER, SPINE, BACK BY

KAY SIMONE

AT

KAY SIMONE CREATIVE

QUOTES OF INSPIRATION

"It is better to be hated for what you are than to be loved for something you are not."– *Andre Gide*

DEDICATION

To those who have to hide.

May you be free to be *you*.

INTRODUCTION

I fell in love with the male/male romance genre back when I wrote my first one (<u>Sawyer, Torey Hope: The Later Years</u>) and couldn't wait to write the six books in my male/male romance series <u>Something About Him</u>. As the most recent series was coming to an end, I started to wonder just what I would write next.

I grew up in small farming community with a railroad running only about 4 houses down from where I lived, so small towns and railroads are familiar to me. My mind started playing with the idea of these three men (Micah, his cousin Levi, and their best friend Cody) growing up on a hill in this small railroad town. *Blueridge* was the name that came to me. Well, then my head started playing with words and landed on nicknaming the series The BJ Boys, so I created Blueridge Junction and the rest is history.

These three stories combine some of my very favorite male/male romance tropes.

In Micah and Cole's story (<u>Fight for It</u>) we find a mechanic and a teacher in an out-for-you tale.

<u>Can't Fight It</u> is a story of opposites attract and May/December romance.

<u>Bound to Fight</u> combines the best of leather daddies and enemies-to-lovers for a great story.

CAST OF CHARACTERS

Micah Edwards- Mechanic in Blueridge Junction, cousin of Levi, best friend of Cody.

Cole Pierce- Teacher at the high school

Levi Wells- Tattoo artist in Blueridge Junction, cousin of Micah, best friend of Cody

Jay Owens- Dancer at Strip Teaze, much younger than the rest of the guys

Cody Parker- Manages his family-owned restaurant/bar (BJ's Burgers & Beer or the B & B) Friends with Levi and Micah

Kennedy Marks- Local police officer in Blueridge Junction

PROLOGUE

MICAH EDWARDS

"What's your name?" I kissed along his strong jawline loving the rough stubble abrading my lips.

He pushed me away, breathless. "No, I told you, no names."

"We've fucked each other's brains out all night long on three separate occasions. I'm assuming tonight will be no exception." I loosened the rubber band he used to keep his shoulder-length blond hair pulled back. Rubbing my hands through the silky locks, I massaged the back of his head. "I told you my name, what's the harm in telling me yours?" Knowing I wouldn't get an answer no matter how often I asked, I pulled him close for another kiss, while coaxing his mouth open with my tongue.

He melted into the kiss, allowing our tongues to mate in a sensual dance before he jerked away. "No, that was the deal. No names, no strings. I can't risk it." He ran a hand down his face, caught his breath. "Besides, there's no proof that the name you gave me is even your real name. *Mike*."

The name I'd given was close enough to the real thing that I didn't even bat an eye at his accusation. "What's the risk? Neither of us are from around here, we're both consenting adults, and we're not doing anything illegal."

"Look, it's just the way it is. I mean, I'd like to continue this little hookup arrangement we've got going on for as long as it works out for us. But the name thing is a deal-breaker. Take it or leave it." His chin jutted, and I recognized the challenge in his blue eyes.

Not wanting to give up the best sex I'd ever had, I accepted his challenge by stepping closer and grabbing the waistband of his jeans. "Fine. No names." I realized a split second too late that I'd walked right into his suspicion of me using a fake name. "No more wasting time on small talk. Get naked."

I watched as the guy who had to be about the same age as my thirty years began to strip. His shoes were kicked off first. Faded blue jeans that fit him like a damn glove slid over the greatest ass I'd ever seen. A casual black button-up shirt covered way too much of his body, and I bit my lip as he tortuously undid each individual button before sliding the shirt from his shoulders. As he toed off his socks and his eyes never left mine, I gritted my teeth in an attempt to tone down my desire as he palmed his cock through snug-fitting black boxer briefs.

"I feel a little underdressed." Nodding toward my jeans, he waited for me to strip.

Every time we'd met up had been the same. Unexplainable connection, sexual tension that sizzled through the rented room, and a back-and-forth, give-and-take teasing before we would fall into bed in a raging inferno of lust. He set my blood on fire. It had started as a random "swipe right" on the dating app, but after spending a few nights with him, I wanted more.

I lived a good hour away from the hotel we used for our meetups. He'd said he didn't live nearby. But could we ever make a go of whatever I felt between us each time we were together?

Based on the way the guy freaked out about names, I had to assume he was a major closet case. As much as I wanted to be in a solid, loving relationship, I wouldn't go back in the closet for a guy I barely knew. I came out a long time ago, and I was too stubborn and proud to hide my sexuality.

Shaking off the intrusive thoughts, I stepped forward; backing him up until his knees hit the mattress. With a quick yank on my shirt, I ripped it over my head and smiled at the fire I saw in his eyes when he took in my chest. Shoes, socks, and pants were next, and then we were both in just our underwear with rock hard cocks weeping and straining to be freed.

But, who would bend first? Who would make the first move?

He reached both hands toward my chest and lightly grazed my nipples with his thumbs. My hiss of breath must have been enough to spur him into further action, because he pulled my head down for a kiss as he fell onto the bed. From above him, I noticed again that our hair was a similar blond, but I kept mine short while his was much longer. My skin had a more olive tone and his looked as if it would burn easily. My frame, slightly taller, likely only outweighed him by about twenty pounds.

Stripping him of his last layer, I immediately licked his leaking cock before taking him deep in my mouth. Letting go of his shaft, I trailed my tongue up his torso then pulled him into a hungry kiss. When he whimpered against my lips, I recalled how much he loved to taste himself on my mouth. Thumbing through the liquid beading on his dick, I traced my thumb across his full bottom lip before kissing him again.

"What do you want?" I knew, but I enjoyed hearing him say it.

"Fuck me," he begged and thrust against me, his cheeks pink and eyes dark with lust.

"You want it slow and gentle?" I stroked his cock as I teased him with my words.

"No." He ground out while thrusting his cock into my fist.

"Tell me how you want it." I demanded.

"Hard and fast. Fuck me hard."

His words were gasoline to my already burning blood. A fire shot straight to my dick as I ripped off my underwear and dove down to rim his ass. Licking, thrusting, tasting, my tongue went to work loosening his tight hole.

Tongue first then my lubed fingers worked in tandem to ready his body before I eased back, rolled the condom down my length, and lined up with his body. "Ready?" I bit out, fighting the urge to slam my cock deep inside him.

He pressed his ass against my dick and moaned. "Yes, just do it. Fuck me."

Giving in to his words, I pulled his calves up to rest on my shoulders before pushing my cock into his ass. "You like that? You want it harder?" As much as I longed to know his name, fucking a stranger was damn hot and had my body shaking with the need to spill myself in him.

He whimpered again, maneuvered so his legs were wrapped around my waist, and then pulled me deeper. "God, yeah, fuck me. Hard."

Rocking into his body, I grabbed his cock and began to stroke.

"Roll over," he gasped, pressing against my chest.

I fought against my body's protest as I slid from his slick hole. Rolling to my back, I held my cock as he positioned himself and slid down my length. Back inside his tight heat, I pumped hard and fast while watching in greedy anticipation as he stroked his cock.

"I want to come," he whined, still stroking himself wildly.

"Do it, come on me." I wanted him to paint my stomach, to give me something if I couldn't know his name. Grabbing his hips, I thrust up over and over until I felt his warm release splatter all over my chest. Watching him empty himself onto my body brought my own release, and I moaned as I filled the condom deep inside his ass.

As seconds turned to moments, our bodies parted long enough for me to dispose of the condom and grab a towel to clean up. Then, we were back together in the standard king-sized hotel bed where I would hold him close until the next round. Times like this made me think we could possibly have more than just random weekly hookups. "I think we should do this more often," I hedged, using two fingers under his chin to pull him in for a slow, deep kiss.

"As long as our time together is anonymous, we can do this as often as you like." His voice held an edge of determination to keep whatever this was hidden.

So, I resolved to keep myself detached. I wanted more with a man, but never if our relationship had to be a dirty little secret.

CHAPTER 1

MICAH

"Are you ready?" My best friend's little sister, Sadie, huffed as she tapped her foot outside the bathroom door at my house. "I swear you take longer than any girl to get ready."

"It takes time to look as good as I do," I teased. "Actually, scrubbing the grease from underneath my fingernails takes a long time. You wouldn't want a grease monkey showing up to your school's Open House, would you?"

"Ew, no. You're not really wearing coveralls are you?"

"No, I only wear those to work...*and* if I think some guy with a mechanic kink would like them. Tonight, I promise to look presentable." Sadie sighed and I inwardly chuckled. I put the finishing touches on my hair and walked into the kitchen with Sadie following.

My family's house in Blueridge Junction had been here for several generations and I loved it. Nestled on Blueridge Hill—the actual hill the town was named after—the Edwards homestead shared the land with only two other properties/families. My cousin, Levi Wells's family had lived in Blueridge as long as we had. And Cody and Sadie Parker's family was almost as native to Blueridge as we were.

We traveled down Blueridge Hill into the town of Blueridge Junction in Colchester County. Blueridge Junction was a sleepy little railroad town in the southern hills of Indiana.

"So, exactly *why* are you dragging Levi, Cody, and me to your Open House?" I grabbed my keys and nodded toward the front door. I'd promised Sadie a ride down the hill and we'd pick up Levi at his tattoo shop on the way. Cody would meet us at the school once he finished up at the restaurant his family had owned for several years.

"I don't know. Just thought it would be nice for some of my family to see the school and meet the teachers." Sadie shrugged in a way that told me her real reason wasn't so nonchalant.

"Mmm hmm, seems strange that this is your senior year and you've never, *not once*, shown any interest in the three of us going to an Open House. What gives?" I studied her long black curls. When her bright green eyes wouldn't meet my gaze, my suspicions were confirmed.

"Fine!" Sadie rolled her eyes and sighed. There's a drop dead gorgeous new teacher this year. He's absolutely bring-you-to-your-knees hot."

"And? You think having your brother and his best friends with you will make a teacher decide to date a student?" I shot her a look of disbelief. *What the hell? I'd known Sadie since she was a baby and now she was after a teacher? Fuck no.*

"No...," she drawled in a sing-songy voice. "I have no proof and not a single girl in school would ever accept my theory, but *I* am of the belief that Mr. Pierce is playing for your team."

"Again, *and*?" I didn't need my best friend's little sister hooking me up, but I sighed inwardly that she wasn't chasing after her teacher.

"I figured either you or Levi might want to take a gander and see if he's your type." Sadie shrugged and batted her lashes.

Crossing the tracks, I rounded the corner and pulled up at Levi's shop. Putting the truck into park, I turned to face Sadie. "You're bringing us along to scope out your new male teacher who you think *may* be gay?"

Sadie nodded with an excited grin. I rolled my eyes, prepared to explain to Sadie why her plan sucked, but I saw Levi heading our way.

Levi walked from the shop and climbed into the truck. He always smelled of rubbing alcohol and soap due to sterilizing his machines and washing up.

"Tell me again why we're going to an Open House? I didn't even attend those things when I was an actual student." Levi grumbled.

I swear, the man was one of my best friends as well as my cousin, but he needed to get laid. Levi had been a grump for months. "Yeah, Sadie, go ahead and tell Levi *why* we're going to the school." I put the truck into gear and headed toward Blueridge Junction High School.

"Shit, Sadie, what kind of scheme are you cooking up now?" Levi's question had merit; Sadie was always setting up things and making plans.

"There's a gorgeous new teacher at school, and I think he may be gay. So, I figured you two could check him out and may the best man win," Sadie quipped.

Levi rubbed a hand over his face. "Jesus, Sade, I mean I appreciate you trying to get us all married, but you can't expect Micah and me to walk in there and inspect the man like he's a side of beef. And then, what? We throw down right then and there? Fight to the finish to see who deserves him? Your heart is good, your intentions are in the right place, but you need to think things through sometimes."

"I'm not saying you're going to take him home and have relations tonight." Sadie rolled her eyes, and I snorted at her choice of words. "I'm just saying that I'm sure he would like to meet new people and you two pretty much only hang out with each other and Cody, so it wouldn't hurt for you three to have more friends your age."

"Does big brother Cody know why you're dragging us all to the school?" I asked as we pulled into the school parking lot where Cody was waiting for us near the front doors of the school. "And are you trying to set him up with the new teacher, too? Maybe we should just have a foursome so no one feels left out?"

Sadie watched her brother as he glowered at Kennedy Marks, one of only a few local law enforcement officers in Blueridge Junction. "No, you guys know Cody is so hung up on Kennedy he'd never go for the new teacher. And, please, no more mention of you three involved in group sex. I've heard enough about that to last me a lifetime."

Levi laughed as we got out of the truck. "What? *You* were the one who asked how we all ended up figuring out the others were gay. The story had to be told."

"La-la-la-la." Sadie stuck her fingers in her ears to block out Levi's words.

I laughed at the memory. The first time Cody had allowed his little sister to join us at a summer bonfire. She'd sat in front of the fire and boldly broached the subject of the three of us being gay.

"How in the world did cousins and best friends all end up gay? And how did you figure it out about each other?" Sadie sipped a nasty beer Cody had purposely given her in hopes of discouraging her from drinking for a while longer.

The three of us had laughed as we recalled the day we figured out we were all gay.

"Well, Cody and Micah had been playing tonsil hockey and practicing their sword swallowing in the locker room one day after track practice. I happened to walk in. Got caught watching, joined in the fun, and the rest is history." Levi shrugged as if the story was as simple as that.

"God, that sounds like a bad porn movie." Sadie wrinkled her nose. "You sucked your cousin's dick?"

"God, no." I shuddered. "Levi and I have never hooked up."

"But you've both hooked up with Cody?" Sadie looked as if she was going to be sick.

"A couple times until we figured out what we were doing. Been a long time since those days, huh?" I swigged my beer and laughed with my best friends.

"Damn, we were horny little bastards back then." Cody smiled and sighed.

"Were? Speak for yourself. I'm still a horny bastard." I waggled my brows.

"No, stop. No more." Sadie held up her hands. "From here on out, I don't want to hear about your sex lives ever again, especially if it includes my brother."

From the bonfire on, we had used the info to taunt Sadie whenever the mood struck.

As we walked to the school's main doors, Sadie unplugged her ears and turned to face us as Cody joined the group. "Seriously, I know Cody only has eyes for Kennedy," she began.

"I can't stand Kennedy Marks," Cody barked a little too loudly. His outburst earned him a scowl from Officer Marks who patrolled the sidewalk a few feet away. Cody gritted his teeth and turned back to Sadie. "We hate each other. End of story."

Sadie rolled her eyes. "Whatever you say." She looked at Levi and me. "But, check out hot teacher guy, see if you get the gay vibe. You don't have to make a move tonight, just feel it out."

Levi and I shook our heads at Sadie's usual matchmaking tactics. There weren't a whole lot of people in Blueridge Junction. As far as I knew, Cody, Levi, and I were three of only five "out" men in town. I suspected a few closet cases, but they were all a lot older than me. Hence, my preferred random hookups outside of Blueridge.

"If he's *really* hot, do you want to play rock, paper, scissors to see who gets to take him home?" I joked with Levi.

"Sure. But, I gotta tell you, I could get all kinds of kinky with some teacher roleplaying." Levi laughed.

"You guys are impossible." Sadie huffed as she threw open the door. "Just shut up, enjoy the cookies and juice and see what you think about Mr. Pierce."

As my eyes adjusted to the inside lighting, I scanned the crowd. Some of the teachers had been teaching at BJHS for over a decade ago. The school building was the same, but some refurbishing had given it a more modern feel. As Sadie rushed to join her gang of friends, Levi, Cody, and I greeted people we knew and headed toward the refreshments.

"Cody, could I talk to you for a minute?" Kennedy Marks's deep voice asked softly.

Cody clenched his jaw, but stalked off with Kennedy to talk about whatever they needed to discuss.

"Heeeey." The lyrical voice greeted us, and Levi closed his eyes as if steeling himself against an attack.

I glanced at my cousin, curious over his distress before addressing the young man who had spoken. "Evening, Jay. How's it going?"

Jay Owens was a walking stereotype of a gay man. Campy, flashy, flamboyant—and absolutely gorgeous. He worked at the local gay bar on the outskirts of town, Strip Teaze, as a dancer. Jay moved to Blueridge Junction at the tender age of eighteen after he fled a less-than-positive home life. Jay had followed Levi around like a lovesick puppy for two years, batting his kohl-lined eyes and pouting his perfect pink pucker in hopes of catching Levi's eye.

"It's great, Micah. Just wanted to come visit the school, see if it was as terrible as I remembered." Jay grinned before gathering up six cookies in napkins and stuffing them in his pockets. "And maybe take advantage of the free snacks."

I caught his guilty blush. My heart went out the kid. He'd lived here for two years, but at the age of twenty he didn't seem to be doing all that great on his own. Jay was slightly built, almost wispy, and looked as if he hadn't had a good meal in ages. Watching him stuff cookies in his pocket, I figured he had come to the open house to scrounge for supper.

"We're going over to BJ's B & B after this. Want to go with us?" I surprised myself by asking. Levi's harsh intake of breath indicated he was just as surprised.

"Yeah? Sure, I'd love to." Jay's eyes brightened and I could almost see the skinny kid salivating at the thought of a real meal.

"Sounds good." I checked my watch. "Meet us out front in about thirty minutes."

I watched Jay all but skip away.

Levi growled, "What the fuck did you just do?"

"Invited a hungry and probably lonely kid to eat dinner with us." I barely stopped myself from adding,

"Duh" to my words. "Why? We were going to eat anyway, what's it matter?"

Levi stared hard at me for a moment before taking a deep breath. "Doesn't matter. Forget I mentioned it."

I was distracted from the conversation by whispers, giggles, and sighs from the female students in attendance. Glancing away from Levi to see what the commotion was about, I felt as if I'd been punched in the gut. There, not even twenty feet away, was my nameless guy.

The best sex partner of my life.

The man I imagined having *more* with.

The guy who refused to disclose his name.

The one who wanted to keep what was between us hidden.

He was the new Social Studies teacher? Sadie had called him Mr. Pierce, and I found it hurt that my best friend's little sister knew his name before I did. *And* I found my gut churned at the thought of her sitting in his class day after day when I only got him once every week or so.

I knew the moment he recognized me because his face went ashen then took on a green tint as if he was trying not to vomit. He looked around wildly as if looking for a quick escape route.

Taking a step toward him, I immediately stopped at the quick shake of his head, warning me away. This wouldn't be a meet-and-greet of two men who had shared many hot, steamy nights. *Mr. Pierce* was making very clear he wanted nothing to do with me, at least in public.

I clenched my jaw and gave him a small nod of understanding before walking away. Something drew me to that man. Something caught in my gut each time I thought of him, but I wouldn't hide myself for him.

How the hell had he ended up in Blueridge Junction?

CHAPTER 2

COLEMAN PIERCE

Fuck my life.

I'd moved to one of the most unknown, out-of-the-way towns in America in order to start over, teach a subject I love, and escape the ugliness of my past.

And the one guy I can't get out of my fucking mind lives here?

Fuck. My. Life.

"Mr. Pierce, I'd like to introduce you to some of Blueridge Junction's original families." Mr. Sutton, the principal, motioned me toward him.

Mike was standing nearby along with two other devastatingly handsome men. The last thing in the world I wanted was walk over and speak to them, but my boss was waiting. No way to gracefully escape existed. Steeling myself against whatever was about to play out, I plastered on a smile and joined Mr.

Sutton. So much for keeping distance between us until I could escape.

"Micah, gentlemen, I'd like to introduce you to Coleman Pierce, Blueridge Junction's newest social studies teacher. Coleman, this is Micah Edwards and his cousin, Levi Wells. Cody Parker completes this little trio. They've been inseparable since birth." Mr. Sutton puffed out his chest as he made introductions.

"Coleman Pierce, nice to put a name with the face," Micah taunted, arching his left brow.

Micah. The name fit him. *Micah.* It became a chant in my head. I'd shared more nights of passion and lust with this man than with any in my entire life. He haunted my dreams. He made me want things I could never want again. And now, he had a name. And he lived in the same town as me. Or, I guess I lived in the same town as him. Either way, fuck my life.

"Dude, you mean a face with a name, right? Cody's little sister, Sadie has been going on and on about *Mr. Pierce* ever since the school year started. Nice to meet you." Levi shook my hand.

"Yeah, yeah, my bad," Micah agreed, but I knew the mix up of words hadn't been a mistake.

"I go by Cole," I said, shaking each man's hand and trying not to visibly shiver when Micah's touch sent a jolt of lust straight through me. "Nice to meet all of you." My voice cracked, but I hoped no one noticed.

"Cole. Got it." Micah's grin was wicked and it did terrible things to my insides. Wonderful, hot, delicious things.

"So, social studies, huh?" Cody's question pulled me back to the conversation.

"Yeah, b-best subject ever...uh...in my opinion." Why was I stuttering and tripping all over my words? I taught classes filled with thirty students. I should be able to speak to three men about my chosen profession. But the heat coming from Micah was short-circuiting my brain. "Um, so, what do you guys do?"

"I manage my family's restaurant and bar, BJ's Burgers & Beer." Cody threw a thumb over his shoulder in the direction of the establishment

"BJ's B & B? Yeah, I've seen it and heard tell of the great food." I nodded.

"It's not the *only* place to eat in town, but it's got the best food and great prices. Plus, the atmosphere is very open and friendly."

Why would Cody throw in that part about open and friendly? Open to what? Friendly to whom? Was Cody implying something? Had Micah said something? No, he hadn't even known my name. Shit, I would end up with a damn ulcer. "I'll definitely have to come try it. I don't do much cooking, so good food at a good price is right up my alley. How late are you open?" I wondered if I could grab something to go that evening. I still had papers to grade after Open House.

"Open every day, ten in the morning to ten at night for food. Bar is open five p.m. to two a.m. We are open for lunch on Sunday, but we close after three p.m."

The info pretty much went over my head because my attention was focused on keeping my gaze from straying to Micah. "Closed on Sundays for church?" I asked the first question that came to mind not really even caring if it made sense.

The three men snorted, and Mr. Sutton huffed and walked away.

"Yeah, something like that." Cody grinned.

I definitely missed an inside joke, but I was too overwhelmed to think about it.

"What about you?" I turned toward Levi. Would I need to ask Micah what he did, or would it be okay to just skip him? *Too obvious, right?*

"I'm the best tattoo artist in town." Levi's face held a smug grin.

"He's the *only* tattoo artist in town," Cody interjected. "But, he truly is the best."

"Ah, good to know," I sputtered and took in the ink that filled Levi's arms. The designs and colors were beautiful. "If I ever decide I want a tattoo, I'll know where to go."

And then an awkward and very obvious lull occurred. Turning to Micah and asking a casual question would have made the most sense, but I was frozen. My brain wouldn't work, body wouldn't move, and words wouldn't come.

Levi gave me a strange look before glancing at his cousin. Clearing his throat, he broke the silence. "And Micah here is a mechanic. Works at his family's shop."

I darted a glance at Micah, nodding my head briefly. "So, I can get food, ink, and an oil change. Sounds like I'm set. Who knew Blueridge Junction would have so many luxuries?"

The men laughed. Well, Levi and Cody laughed. Micah remained quiet.

"Yeah, old BJ has pretty much everything we need." Cody's use of the town's initials confused me for a second before my brain caught up. "Didn't always used to be that way. But, traveling to the bigger towns got expensive and wasn't convenient, so people started setting up shop here. After a while, we got some extras. Used to be, people moved away from BJ as soon as they were old enough. But now, many choose to stay. It's a great place to live."

"How long have you been here?" Levi tossed another glance at Micah before turning his attention to my answer.

"I'm not even officially moved in. Driving an hour each way every day was going to suck and add wear and tear on my already beat up car, so Mr. Sutton let me sleep at the school most of this week. I'll drive back this weekend and load up my car. Should be able to move into the apartment on Saturday." I was really looking forward to having a place to call my own. I'd be sleeping on the carpet in my apartment until I could buy a couch or mattress, but at least I wouldn't be squatting at the school and taking showers in the locker room. Plus, Mr. Sutton had been *very* clear that staying at the school was a limited time offer.

"Well, be sure to give us a holler if you need help with anything." Levi nodded out the window toward the hill that towered in the distance. "The three of us live up on Blueridge Hill. We're the only houses up there, so you'll be able to find one of us no matter which house you pick."

"Okay, that sounds good. Thanks." No way in hell did I plan on calling any of them. I needed to keep my distance. Levi and Cody seemed nice enough, but Micah was my Kryptonite. I couldn't allow myself to get close to him. The draw was too strong. If I was going to keep my secret, I *had* to stay away from Micah.

"We're heading to grab dinner, want to join us?" Levi asked but his attention was turned toward Micah. Levi and Cody seemed to be studying him, but Micah only furrowed his brow before frowning at his friends.

"Ah, thanks, but no. I need to get some papers graded after this event is over." My stomach rumbled in protest, but I had some protein bars to hold me over until I could get moved into my apartment and buy some groceries. I'd get takeout some other night—when Micah wasn't around.

"Suit yourself." Levi shrugged. "Good to meet you."

Micah seemed to come out of his trance and he reached for my hand. When our skin met, I gasped as electric shocks sparked between us again. "Great meeting you, *Cole*. Looking forward to seeing you around town. Let me know if you need help getting settled."

The heat in his touch, the fire in his eyes, and the promise in his words threatened to undo me. I didn't hear a word of what Cody and Levi said as they departed.

My boss had been hovering at the edge of the little meet-and-greet, but once they left, he returned to my side. "That went well. You'll need to become friends with those three if you want to fit in here. The Edwards, Wells, and Parker names are held in high regard. I can't say I approve of everything those boys do, but their families rule this town. Founding fathers type stuff." Mr. Sutton rattled on, but I could concentrate on nothing more than Micah's perfect ass as he walked away. And on how the hell I was going to make it in Blueridge Junction with Micah Fuckin' Edwards as one of the Golden Boys.

Fuck. My. Life.

CHAPTER 3

MICAH

"What the hell were you doing inviting him to dinner?" I rounded on Levi as soon as we were out of the building.

"Whoa, man. Chill out." Levi protested. "What? *You* can invite anyone you want to eat with us, but I can't extend the same invite to the new guy in town?"

His question rankled me. "Got the hots for him?" I challenged even though I knew I sounded like a brat.

"No, didn't feel a spark between us, but he seems like a nice guy. He seemed lonely. Thought it would be a nice gesture." Levi shrugged. "Since we're on the subject though, why are you so damn prickly? *You* have the hots for him?"

My cousin had no clue. Hot for *Cole*—finally a damn name—didn't even begin to describe what I felt. Desire, longing, anger, confusion, and yes, definitely hot.

"Still want to take me to dinner, daddy?" Jay saved me from having to answer Levi by strutting up at that exact moment.

"Damnit, Jay, don't call me that," Levi growled.

"It's a term of endearment." Jay pouted, batting lashes anyone would die for. "Means I like you." Jay blew a kiss to Levi, and Cody and I busted out laughing.

"It's inappropriate," Levi snapped. "I'm thirty fuckin' years old. You're barely legal."

"I'm almost twenty-one," Jay corrected.

"Doesn't matter. Even if I *wanted* something to happen between us—which I don't—you are *way* too young and definitely not my type." Levi's words were harsher than I thought they needed to be, and I winced at the wounded look on Jay's face.

Drawing in a deep breath, Jay seemed to fortify himself. "Fine, whatev. I like a challenge." Jay put a hand on the back of Levi's neck and stood on his tiptoes to whisper loudly in Levi's ear. "I'll wear you down, bit by bit, daddy. You won't be able to resist me forever."

"Watch me." Levi turned, walked toward BJ's Burgers & Beer, and then shot a glance over his shoulder. "I'll meet you guys there."

"I've never seen someone get under Levi's skin the way you do, kid." I slapped Jay on the back and motioned toward my truck.

"It's my specialty. I tend to annoy the fuck out of most people," Jay quipped.

His words were careless, but I suspected Levi's cold shoulder hurt more than the young man let on.

"And, how ironic that *I* get under the skin of Mr. Badass Tattoo Artist? You know, with *him* putting ink under people's skin for a living."

We'd covered the few blocks to BJ's B&B so I just smirked at Jay's comment as we got out of the truck.

Cody had a table ready for us when we walked in. Levi entered behind us, scowling for all he was worth. As I sat down, I couldn't stop thinking about Cole. Jay was grinning ear-to-ear, seemingly oblivious to the tension around him. The kid's tongue nearly fell out of his mouth when he began scanning the menu. Knowing Jay didn't have much money, I put him out of his misery. "Get whatever you want, it's on me." I gestured toward the menu.

Levi put his head in both hands and groaned.

"What? I can't treat? Fine, you can buy." I tossed a straw paper at him.

"It's like feeding a damn stray cat," Levi mumbled. "Now he'll never leave."

I glared at my cousin. "No need to be rude." Glancing at Jay, though, I saw the kid was too busy making dinner decision to care about what Levi said.

Cody walked over and plopped down three plates of appetizers. "Dinner's on the house, men. Eat up."

Jay shoveled food in his mouth.

"Anything you don't eat can be boxed up and taken home for leftovers."

I knew right then and there that Cody would make sure Jay took home a week's worth of leftovers. Levi simply shook his head in defeat.

The next hour was spent dividing my time between watching Jay eat like he'd not had a good meal in years, laughing at the constant quarrel among Jay and Levi about a tattoo—Jay wanted Levi to ink him, Levi refused until Jay was at least twenty-one and maybe not even then— and thinking about Cole. The man hadn't left my mind for more than a moment or two since our last hookup. How the hell was I supposed to live in the same town as him if he wouldn't give me the time of day outside of a hotel room?

Recalling Jay's words from earlier, I let the beginnings of a plan start to grow in my head. Cole wouldn't be able to resist me forever. Could he? I could wear him down bit by bit, right? Did I really have it in me to fight for a man who was determined to never come out of his hiding place?

~*~*~

Two weeks later, I concluded Cole was a lost cause. The texts I'd sent him daily had been completely ignored. The phone calls I'd made went straight to voicemail—and I'd stopped leaving messages a couple days after I realized how pathetic I sounded.

The harshest punch to the stomach was when Cole blocked me on the dating app.

I didn't even see him around town. I heard people talk about him. Sadie went on and on about Mr. Pierce and how much she loved his class. Cody said he'd seen Cole in BJ's Burgers & Beer several times getting two lunches to go which meant he was buying lunch for someone else, or he was taking the extra home for dinner.

Hell, even my own parents saw Cole more than I did.

"Saw that damn sissy school teacher in town again today. Driving a piece of shit car, wearing that punk girly ponytail, in those fuckin' *skinny leg* pants of his," Dad groused at the dinner table. "Don't know what the damn school board was thinking hiring the likes of him."

"The students seem to like him, and he was obviously qualified." Mom spoke softly.

Didn't matter how many times I reminded Dad that Levi, Cody, and I were gay, he refused to accept it, acknowledge it, or speak of it. But he had no problem gouging me over and over with his diatribe about other men he assumed were gay.

"Town doesn't need faggots running the place. We need real men to take over when us old timers retire." Dad waved his fork around, gravy dripping from a chunk of beef. "Upstanding, responsible, respectable men like your brother, Mitch, and Kennedy Marks."

Dad would shit a brick if he ever found out Officer Kennedy Marks was gay. How he hadn't figured it out yet was beyond me. Guess he just didn't see anything stereotypically gay about Kennedy.

And Mitch. Good old Mitch. Big brother extraordinaire. We'd never really been close, even as kids. Mitch had absolutely no interest in taking over the mechanic shop when Dad retired, but that didn't matter to Dad. The man would turn the business over to Mitch just to spite me. Passive aggressive piece of shit.

My dad knew I wanted to take over the shop. I'd been planning on it since I was old enough to change oil and replace a flat. But, Dad didn't approve of my sexuality. His constant hateful comments regarding other gay men and his desire to give the shop to Mitch hurt me every time.

I excused myself from the table, put my dishes in the sink, kissed my momma on the cheek, and headed toward my truck. I had to be at the shop early in the morning, but I refused to hang around and be shamed by my father. The best thing about the three houses on Blueridge Hill was they all had guesthouses. Levi had moved into the main house when his parents died. Cody and I still lived in the guesthouses on our parents' property.

In my truck, I pulled up to Cody's house without much thought on my part. Levi was an only child and his parents died when he was a senior in high school. My mom was okay, but my dad was shit. Cody's parents had supported the three of us since before we'd even realized we were gay. Hank and Marian were more *there* for me than my parents ever had been.

"Daddy dearest being a prick?" Hank asked from his spot on the swing as I climbed the steps to the Parker's front porch.

"As usual," I replied. "Cody home?"

"Should be soon. Grab a beer." Hank nodded his head toward the door. "Marian is inside, she'd love to see you."

By the time Cody got home, Hank and I were laughing at memories of Levi, Cody, and me as youngsters.

"Good seeing you, Micah." Hank stood from the porch swing. "It's my bedtime. I've got to open the restaurant tomorrow. No good dirty rotten manager I hired thinks he needs to come in late after his closing shifts." Hank chucked Cody on the shoulder before retiring inside for the night.

Cody popped inside the house before returning with two more beers. "What's up man?" He motioned toward the yard, and we walked toward the stream where we used to play as kids.

"Nothing much. Just wanted to get out of the house. Dad was going on and on about that new teacher. Then he started in on how Mitch was the best choice for taking over the shop. Too early to go to bed, so I went for a drive." I shrugged and swigged my beer. *And, if I went to bed this early, I'd just end up jerking off to images of Cole.*

"You ever think we could do better than Blueridge Junction?" Cody asked out of the blue.

I studied my best friend's face and thought about his question. "Not sure. I mean, I'm sure we could be successful in many places. And sometimes I think it would be nice to live in a bigger city. More people, more options, just *more*. But, overall, I like what we've got here. I don't think I'd want to leave." My heart thumped wildly as I wondered what had brought on the question. "Why, you thinking of leaving?"

Cody sipped his beer silently for a few moments. "Not really." He sighed. "I mean, I think it'd be nice to see the vast variety the world has to offer outside of Blueridge Junction." He threw a twig in the water. "I feel like it would be so much easier sometimes to be in a big city. More anonymity, more acceptance, just *more*. I mean, I don't feel like the three of us hide who we really are, but sometimes it feels like we can't *truly* be who we really are."

I thought about his words. "I mean, you have your Sundays at the bar. That's something you wanted and you made it happen. If I remember correctly you didn't give a damn about what the town said. I mean, it's not like you're plastering the town with advertisements of the event, but it brings people in."

"Yeah, I know. And I appreciate that." Cody finished his beer. "I guess sometimes I just wish we were in a place where we weren't being studied so much. Feels like there's always someone watching and judging."

"Yeah, I get that." And I did understand exactly what Cody was saying. "But, this is our home. The town was built by our ancestors. Our families *are* Blueridge Junction."

We watched a cloud tease the edge of the moon before Cody turned a shit-eating grin my way. "Damn straight we are. And *we're* the fucking BJ Boys."

"Not sure straight's the right word," I joked.

Cody and I spent the next thirty minutes shootin' the shit before I said I needed to head home. "Gotta be at the shop early in the morning." I slapped him on the back. "Thanks for the beer. Tell Hank and Marian goodnight for me."

That night, same as all the other nights since meeting Cole Pierce, I dreamed of him.

"Need you to tow a car in," Dad hollered from the office.

"I'm up to my elbows in grease, can't one of the other guys do it?" I pressed away from the vehicle I was working on.

"I'm still in charge around here, and I said I want *you* to tow the car in." Dad threw a paper airplane at me before he slammed his office door. Before I could even wipe my hands on a towel, Dad yanked the door back open. "And the customer is waiting with the car. Don't make 'em wait."

Cleaning my hands the best I could, I grabbed a couple waters and headed toward the tow truck. Unfolding the piece of paper, I checked the address. No GPS was needed, I knew Blueridge Junction like the back of my hand, although the customer had broken down almost as far away from town as possible.

I reached the broken-down car on a deserted stretch of road between BJ and the next town over. Pulling up behind the junky vehicle, I laughed out loud and felt my heart beat rapidly.

Cole Fuckin' Pierce was standing next to the car.

I slid from the cab of the tow truck. "Cole. Fancy meeting you here." I sauntered toward the man and smiled when he realized *I* was the one who had come to rescue him.

"Fuck my life," Cole mumbled.

"What was that?" I couldn't keep the laughter from my voice.

"Nothing." Cole huffed. "Are you the only tow truck in town?"

"Yes, sir'ee." I held out my hand. "Micah Edwards of Ed's Autos at your service."

"Damn it. Stupid phone barely gets service out here. I about used up all my damn data looking up the closest repair shop. Should've known it would be you." Cole grumbled.

"Well, if you want to get technical. My father, Ed Edwards, took your call. He just sent me out to tow you in." I wasn't mad at dear old dad for sending me out on the call. Not mad at all.

"Whatever. Let's just get the car towed into town." Cole reached into his pocket for his keys and then looked forlornly at the boxes in the backseat. "Can the boxes ride back there?"

"Sure. Not a problem. I can swing by your place to drop off the boxes and you before I take your car to the shop." While I was frustrated with Cole, I wouldn't be a dick about things.

Cole stuttered and shuffled his feet. "Um, so, how much do you think it will be to fix the car?"

Fighting not to roll my eyes, I took pity on the guy. "Depends on what's wrong with it. No way to know until I get under her and check things out." I started hooking up the car to the truck. "First tow into town is free." That wasn't the truth, but I wouldn't make Cole pay. Fate had led me out to him, and I wasn't going to tempt fate by making him pay. No, I'd just tempt my father's anger by not charging for a service. "I'll take a look at the car and figure out what's wrong. Then, I'll have a better idea of what the parts and service will cost."

Cole nodded in defeat. "So, um, if you find out what's wrong with it and I can't afford to have it fixed, how much will the bill be?"

Money was clearly tight.

"Too soon to tell. Let's just get you back into town and the car up on the block. I'll be able to tell you more once I get a good look under her hood." I had the car hooked up and ready. "Come on, hop in." I gestured toward the passenger door of the tow truck.

When Cole came to the door, I knew I had a decision to make. Play it cool and go easy on Cole like I was perfectly fine with the way things had played out. *Or.* Or, I could lay it all out for him. Grill him. Put him on the spot. Let him know I wasn't okay with the way things had gone down.

With a wide-open field at my back, and the truck between us and the empty road, I stepped forward and pinned Cole against the door. "I've tried texting and calling, *Cole*." The heat of the day surrounded us, but the heat that sizzled between our bodies was almost painful.

"I've been busy with school and moving and…," Cole's excuses trailed off as I nibbled on his ear.

"So, once you're moved and settled in, you'll take my calls? Respond to my texts? Unblock me on the dating app?" My lips tingled as they brushed against his stubbly jawline. I tasted the faint saltiness of sweat upon his skin. Cole's head fell back against the truck window, allowing me access to his neck and throat. I'd missed this, I'd missed *him*. "Answer me, Cole." But, I didn't give him much chance to answer as I kissed and nibbled along his neck.

Cole rocked against me, breathing heavily when I caught his hips in my hands and held him still so I could thrust my cock roughly against his. "Micah, stop. We can't do this out here. Someone will see."

His words lit a fire to my anger while dousing my desire with ice water.

"So, you're still up for hookups as long as they remain secret and hidden?" I bit out the question even as I already knew the answer.

"More so now than ever." Cole's breathing was ragged. His lips plump. His skin flushed. He looked one hundred percent fuckable. "I'm a teacher. I can't be out and proud like you. I could lose my job if the people in charge got wind of it."

"Of what? Messing around with me?" I scoffed. "Blueridge Junction fuckin' loves me. You couldn't do much better in the town's eyes."

"Not because of *you*." Cole sighed. "A gay mechanic is one thing. But, very few people in a small town are okay with an educator being gay. You can't turn a car gay by working on it, but I may just turn a student gay by teaching them social studies." Cole's words were bitter.

"You admit you're gay." It wasn't a question.

"Of course I'm gay." Cole rolled his eyes.

"But, you're planning to hide it from the whole town?" My anger fought with my pity for the man.

"It's not a choice. If I want to keep my job, I have to hide it." His jaw clenched as he crossed his arms over his chest.

"For how long?"

"Forever."

My chest ached both at my loss of whatever he and I could have been and his lonely future.

"You're going to deny who you really are for a job?" I couldn't believe what I was hearing.

"You wouldn't understand." Cole shook his head.

I wanted to challenge him. To push him. To force him to tell me more about his ridiculous plan. But, I knew I'd prodded enough right then, so I let it go. "We aren't done talking about this." I tipped up his chin so I could brush a soft kiss against his lips. "And *this* isn't done." I sealed the promise with a final kiss before opening the truck door to help Cole inside.

The ride back to town was fairly quiet. There was much I wanted to say. Much I wanted to ask. But, Cole looked run down, ragged, and ready to drop. "Hey, where's your new place?"

Cole pulled himself from his sleepy trance and faced me. "Oh, um, the apartments behind the park."

I worked to keep the surprise from my face. The four unit building was about as run down as anything a person could find in Blueridge Junction. Why the hell would Cole choose to live there?

"Yeah, I know. Not the best of places, but it's all I could afford for now." Cole read my thoughts as easily as if I'd spoken the words.

"No worries, man." I felt bad for judging. Cole deserved better than a run-down little hole in the wall. I wanted to give him more. Pushing away the thought, I continued. "I know where it's at. I'll get you dropped off and get Bessie here back to the shop."

"Bessie?" Cole smirked.

"Yeah. Bessie. You know, that piece of junk you drive that I'm currently hauling behind us?" I threw my thumb over my shoulder.

"Bessie has served me well for several years I'll have you know." Cole chewed on his bottom lip. "Really hope she's got a few more years left in her."

"If she's fixable, I can fix her." Without thinking, I reached for Cole's hand and squeezed. "Really, I'm the best mechanic in BJ and probably for three counties. I'll get Bessie running again."

Cole let me hold his hand for a few seconds before closing his eyes, taking a deep breath, giving my hand a squeeze, and letting go. I knew letting me go pained him because I was feeling the same when our hands broke apart. I pulled up to his new place. "Want help with the boxes?" I wasn't ready to say goodbye.

Cole likely gave himself whiplash turning to look at me as if I was insane. "No, I'll get them, but thanks." He jumped from the truck and grabbed the boxes from his car. Stacking them on the sidewalk, he came back to the truck. "So, um, yeah. You can call me. About the car." His meaning was clear.

"Oh, I'll call you." My words were meant to sound threatening, and the blanch of Cole's face made it clear *I* had hit my mark too. "Remember, we're not done with our conversation. Or anything else."

"We have to be." Cole straightened from the window. "There's no other choice."

"There's always another choice. You just have to be willing to accept it." I winked and then eased the truck away from the curb.

By the time I got Bessie back to the shop, I breathed a sigh of relief that Dad had left for the day.

Finishing up the car I'd been working on before the call to rescue Cole came through, I called the customer and let them know it was available to pick up. I grabbed a bite to eat and then got Bessie jacked up. "All right, girl. Let's take a looksee at what's troubling you."

I spent the rest of the day and well into the evening absolutely in my element. I had the shop to myself. Music thumping. A car to puzzle over. And thoughts of Cole dancing through my head. Thank you, Dad, for being a lazy, no-good asshole and sending me on a call out.

CHAPTER 4

COLE

"Well, hello there, Mr. Pierce." Jay Owen's perched next to me at the bar where I was waiting on my to-go order.

I'd met Jay through Cody, the owner of BJ's Burgers & Beer where I got seventy-five percent of my meals. A lot of people in town were friendly, welcoming, and perfectly nice. But, somehow, I had managed to land mostly gay men in the majority of my new friends. Birds of a feather, I guess.

"Hi, Jay. And call me Cole. Mr. Pierce seems sort of creepy the way you say it." I was only slightly joking.

"It's supposed to," Jay drawled and winked. "No, but seriously, where's your car? I've seen you walking lately."

"It's in the shop. Broke down on the last trip back from my old place." I checked the time. I had nowhere to be, but chit-chat with Jay rarely stayed neutral.

"*Micah's* working on your car?" Jay's eyes bugged out.

"Yeah, why?"

"Just, if Micah was working on *my* car, I'd be over there from open until close watching." Jay bit his lip.

"You don't have a car, Jay." I rolled my eyes and tried to change the subject.

"Elementary, my dear. You totally know what I mean." Jay fanned himself. "Mmm, just think of Micah all sweaty. Pulling those coveralls down to his waist. Bending over that car just like he'd bend over you."

"Whoa, okay. Calm down there before you work yourself into a froth." I had to laugh at Jay's detailed description.

Cody came over and plopped down my to-go bag. He handed Jay a bag as well. "Here, made too many fries. You can take them."

Jay smiled and grabbed the bag. "Thanks, Papa Bear."

"Call me that again and I'll take them back." Cody flicked a towel at Jay as we walked to the register to pay.

Once out on the sidewalk, Jay and I sauntered toward the park.

"You've got to know that Micah is like majorly hot for you, right?" Jay asked around a mouthful of fries.

"No. He's not. And, even if he was, it wouldn't matter. I'm not looking." The lies rolled from my tongue easier each time I said them.

"Girl, you keep telling yourself that all you want, but I'm telling you. Micah Edwards is totally hot for Cole Pierce." Jay teased. "It's like fate. You end up teaching here. Your car breaks down. Hot-as-sin Micah Edwards comes to rescue you in his big truck. Mmm, I'd let him hoist me up and tow me anywhere he wants."

"Dude, chill out. Micah doesn't like me. I don't like Micah. I'm not looking for anything in the romance department. My job is what's important to me." We had almost reached the park. I'd go one way and Jay would, hopefully, go his own way.

"Only having your job to fulfill you is a sad and lonely way to live. You need friends and love. And sex. Lots of sex." Jay gave a dramatic sigh.

"I'm making friends. I love my job. And sex is overrated." *Lies, lies, lies.*

"Then you're not having it right," Jay quipped.

"Yeah? Who are you having sex with?" I challenged in hopes of changing the subject.

"Me?" Jay put a hand to his chest. "Ladies don't kiss and tell, but I'll have you know I'm saving myself for the right person."

I couldn't help the look of shock on my face. Glancing around, I whispered, "You're a virgin?"

Jay sobered quickly. "Yeah, but can you keep that quiet? I have a reputation to uphold."

"No problem, your secret is safe." I held up my hand in promise.

Jay slung an arm around my neck. "And your secret is safe with me. For now."

Panicked, I pulled away. "What secret?"

Jay smiled sadly. "Cole, you need to start being honest with yourself. No town, no job, nothing is worth being miserable over. Your eyes light up when I even mention Micah. This town may not be the most forward-thinking and open-minded place in the world, but it's not too bad. I mean, Micah, Levi, Cody, and Kennedy all get along just fine here. Yeah, run-of-the-mill homophobes exist here, but if *I* can make it in BJ, anyone can. Don't keep feeding yourself lies. Your *job* isn't going to hold you, kiss you, love you. You need more than that. Don't stay trapped in that self-imposed closet forever. You'll wither away from loneliness and self-hate." Jay twirled around gracefully. "Come out and play! You've got people to support you."

I rolled my eyes and shook my head. "You have no idea what you're talking about. I'm perfectly happy with my life."

Jay's eyes were sad when he cupped my cheek. "I'll forgive you for lying to me. This time. But, pretty soon, you'll have to accept the truth."

That night, I tossed and turned in bed for several hours. Damn Jay and his little speech. I *was* perfectly happy with my life. I loved teaching. I had moved on from some really shitty things that I preferred to keep in the past. I was making a new path for myself.

Yes, I liked Micah Edwards. The sex was amazing, but I liked him for more than just that. But Micah wasn't the type to hide. Micah was brave and courageous and stood up for what he believed in. He wouldn't accept keeping things on the down low. And I couldn't make my sexuality known. End of story.

I'd have to make Micah understand that we either kept things secret and keep hooking up, or we accepted that what we had was over. Could we just be friends? I wasn't sure I was strong enough for that. Could I stand to be around when Micah found someone else?

First thing the next day I would go by the auto shop and check on my car. And, if possible, talk to Micah about…well, talk to him about all the *stuff* we needed to discuss.

CHAPTER 5

MICAH

I felt his presence before he spoke. Thankfully, Dad was locked away in his office, likely sleeping at his desk while he pretended to do paperwork. The arrival of someone at the shop could have been anyone, but somehow, I knew it was Cole.

He cleared his throat. "What's the damage?"

I rolled myself out from underneath the vehicle slowly. Allowing my gaze to travel from Cole's black dress shoes, up his trim-fit pants, to his fitted button-up, before I stopped momentarily at his tie and thought of all the things we could do with that accessory. Not standing from the creeper, I stared up at Cole from flat on my back. In this position, I couldn't stop my mind from wandering to how he'd ridden me on the last night we were together. From the fiery gaze Cole pinned on me, I had a feeling his mind went there as well.

"I'll get you an itemized list of parts and services, but the grand total shouldn't be more than about two hundred." In actuality, the car needed about six hundred dollars worth of work, but I figured Cole's teacher paycheck didn't have much left at the end of the month. I'd charge him for parts, but I would service the car for free in my spare time.

Cole's face was immediately filled with relief. "Whew. I mean two hundred isn't pocket change, but it's doable. That's great to hear. Thanks."

"No worries." I wiped my hands on a shop towel and stood to face Cole. "We're pretty backed up right now, so it may be a few more days until I can get her back to you."

Cole stood chest-to-chest with me for a brief moment before taking a step back. But not before I saw the grit of his jaw and the flutter of his pulse under the soft skin of his neck. "Not a problem. The weather hasn't been bad, so walking isn't an issue. Plus, I don't live far from work or the B & B. Aside from picking up groceries, there's not many other places in town I need to go."

"I can take you to get groceries later." I checked my watch. "Will you be home about six-thirty?"

"I don't need you to take me for groceries." Cole huffed. "In fact, that's what I came here to talk to you about. I mean, other than my car."

"Groceries?" I goaded.

"No." Cole took a deep breath and ran a hand over his face. "Can you take a break so we can talk?" He looked over his shoulder at my dad's office. "In private?"

I narrowed my eyes as I briefly wondered just what Cole wanted to talk about. Gut reaction was that I wouldn't like it. I nodded my head toward the backdoor of the shop. "Sure." I led the way through the bay.

Once outside, I took a seat on top of the picnic table while Cole kept his distance. When he looked at me, I simply raised a brow in question. This was Cole's show for the moment.

"Okay, so, I've been thinking," Cole blurted.

"And?" I had no intention of making the situation easy.

"I would *really* like to continue what we had going before I moved to Blueridge Junction." Cole rushed his words.

"Me too," I drawled.

"Yeah?" Cole's face registered his surprise.

"Definitely." I nodded.

"So, should we keep going to the same hotel or maybe there's a place closer to BJ?"

"There's a place closer. In fact, it's right here in BJ." I gave him a wicked grin. "My bed is right up the hill. Perfect spot."

"No, I thought I made myself clear." Cole crossed his arms. "I can't be seen hooking up with guys. Too many townspeople and school board members would balk at finding out I'm gay."

"And I thought I made myself clear." I stood to use my height to full advantage. "I want you in my life and in my bed. But I won't go back to hiding. We don't have to advertise it, but I'm not sneaking around."

Cole sighed deeply and closed his eyes. "Then I guess we're at an impasse."

"Yeah, I guess we are." I stepped forward, backing him into the wall. "When you figure out you're tired of being alone, come on back." Grazing his jawline with my thumb, I whispered, "I'd love to see what we could become."

Cole's nostrils flared with what appeared to be equal parts desire and anger.

"I'll come back."

My heart stuttered a beat before he continued. "When my car is ready." And with that, he turned and stalked toward the door.

"What are you pansy asses doing out here?" My dad stood in the doorway, blocking Cole's escape. "I don't pay you to have tea and cookies with the likes of him." Dad spoke to me as if Cole wasn't standing right in front of him. "Can't count on you to keep things running right around here. Damn near have to do everything myself if I want it done right." Dad gave Cole an evil eye before retreating back into the shop. "Get back to work, boy!"

My stomach churned. I'd never wanted Cole to be subjected to Dad's hatred. Glancing at Cole, I watched him let out a long breath.

"Sorry about that. Dad's an ass. Always has been, always will be. The Wells and Parker families run Blueridge Junction on respect and mutual admiration. The Edwards family, at least since Dad's generation, got our place through plain old bullying." I watched/studied the empty doorway where my father had been. I truly hated the man. If it wasn't my sexuality he was bitching about, it was something else. He'd never been happy with anything in life. And Mom was almost as bad. I mean, she tried, but she had never once stood up to my dad and spoken her mind. And who knows, maybe she was more in agreement with Dad than I thought. More than once, Cody and Levi and even mere acquaintances had remarked on how amazing it was that I'd turned out pleasant and respectable. I guess I decided early on to model myself as the complete opposite of my father. And I definitely wanted my future relationship to be one hundred percent different than my parents' marriage.

"No. I mean, yes, he's an ass." Cole scowled and shook his head. "But, that right there? The way he acted? *That* is exactly why I can't be out and proud and dating guys." Cole shook his head. "It's just the way it is for me." He turned and walked away.

I stared after him, feeling an ache in my chest. How did I feel such a connection and such a rightness with a guy I barely knew past our great times in bed? It didn't make sense, but something deeper than sex existed between us.

"So, you and Cole, huh?" Jay sauntered into the bay while I was finishing up the last bit of work on Bessie for the day.

I jerked my head toward Dad's office, relieved to find it dark. He must have left while I was working. "No, doesn't look like it." I wrinkled my brow at the kid. "Why?"

"Because it's obvious you two fine men are hot for each other. So, what's the issue?" Jay popped a hip and cocked his head with a heap of sass thrown in for good measure.

"The issue is...," I started, then paused. "Why am I telling you this? It's really none of your business."

"Well, Papi, I happen to know a certain hot-as-fuck social studies teacher was just seen walking into the grocery store. Since his car is here being worked over by your strong and capable hands," Jay batted his lashes and bit his lip, "I thought *maybe* a manly mechanic such as yourself may want to go offer said teacher a ride. In your truck. And later, on your stick shift. If you get my drift."

I took a deep breath. "Yeah, Jay, I get your drift. And don't call me Papi." I put my tools away while

I spoke. "I will deny this if you breathe a word of it to anyone, but that ship has sailed."

Jay crinkled his nose. "You two did the deed and it sucked? Damn, I'm sorry. I didn't see that one coming."

I laughed. "No, it most definitely didn't suck."

"I bet *he* did," Jay teased.

God, the kid made my head spin trying to keep up with him. "I just mean that Cole and I aren't on the same page with where we see things going."

"He wants a white picket fence, butt babies, and a dog?" Jay kept a straight face and blinked his eyes innocently.

I rolled my eyes. "Damn it, Jay. That's ridiculous and you know it. *Butt babies*?" I couldn't help but laugh. "Does Cole seem like the out and proud settle-down-with-my-male-partner type to you?"

Jay huffed but smirked as he relented. "Fine. You got me." Jay looked around as if he was protecting a national secret. "But, I think you can work with that." He nodded smugly.

"Work with what? The fact that he's so far in his closet he'd need a map to get out?" I finished putting my tools away and washed up. My head hurt, because Jay was talking in circles.

"Girl, fine. I can see I'm going to have to spell it out for you." Jay came to lean against the sink while I dried my hands. "Let Cole *think* you're okay with a secret affair."

"What? No way. I'm not hiding." I shook my head. "No fucking way am I going back. I want more for myself. My parents have a terrible relationship. I want real partnership and true love. I'm not going to be someone's dirty secret." Damn, what was it about this kid that made me feel like spilling my guts. "It was hard accepting myself and coming out. I'm not going backwards from that."

"I'm not saying you have to go backwards or deny your true self." Jay clucked his tongue. "Just hear me out."

I rolled my eyes, weary of the conversation and ready for dinner and a beer, but I allowed Jay to continue.

"You like Cole. Cole likes you. You want to be out in the open. Cole would rather be strung up by his nads." Jay gestured with a flourish. "What's going to be easier? Convincing Cole to out himself for a guy he barely knows? *Or* convincing Cole to out himself for a guy he's completely head-over-heels in love with?"

I shoved a hand through my hair. "Option B, obviously. But it's a little hard to get a guy to fall in love with you if they won't give a budding relationship a chance."

"Did Cole *say* he wanted nothing to do with you?" Jay prodded.

"No. He said he wanted nothing to do with me in *public*." I cracked my neck.

"Right. So, let Cole think you're okay with being on the down low for a while. Let him get to know you. Wine him, dine him, sixty-nine him." Jay waggled his beautifully arched brows. "Then, *bam*, once he's fallen for you, he'll have no choice but to out himself for love."

I stared at Jay for several moments while I ran his words through my head. "That's either the most asinine plan I've ever heard..." My words trailed off as I gave the thought more time to simmer.

"Or?" Jay's cheeky smile seemed to challenge me.

I couldn't help but grin and shake my head. "Or, you're an absolute genius."

"I think it's the latter, but only time will tell." Jay shoved a lock of hair from his face.

"You know this could backfire so badly it will be talked about three counties over, right?" I stared at the ceiling as if the right decision was written there.

"It could. But, if you don't give it a chance, you'll still be without Cole. And he'll still be sad and alone with only his social studies to keep him warm." Jay shrugged. "At least this way, you have a *chance* of it working out. Letting Cole go without a fight? That's giving up a possible chance of a lifetime."

"You're right. I'm not giving up without a fight." I checked my phone for the time. "I gotta go."

"Bye, Papi. I'll see myself out." Jay waggled his fingers.

After locking up, I was in my truck and gunning toward the grocery store before my mind could even process a plan. I just knew I would fight for Cole, fight for our *more*. Whether he wanted me to or not.

CHAPTER 6

COLE

"What kind of cereal do you like? Me, I like the more wholesome kinds and then I add fruit and shit to it at home." Micah Fuckin' Edwards stood next to me in the cereal aisle.

I turned to stare. That's all I could do.

When Micah winked at me, I lost it. "What the hell are you doing here?" I hissed, glancing around to be sure no one was within earshot.

"Picking up some necessities." Micah peered into my shopping cart. "Mmm, I love those cookies. Cody's mom always had them around. She'd have tea and cookies while the three of us ate milk and cookies." He shifted the shopping basket on his arm and picked a box of breakfast cereal from the shelf. "Now, Marian's oatmeal cookies were to die for, but when she didn't have the homemade ones, the store-bought ones were the next best thing."

"Why are you here in the store at the exact same time as I am?" I tried to keep calm even though my head and heart were in a screaming war with each other. My head said it was absolutely crazy for Micah to be in the grocery store casually talking as if nothing had happened. My heart was giddy with the thought of shopping with Micah as a real couple someday. But, even if Micah accepted my offer, we'd never be able to stroll through the store picking out groceries.

"Luck? I mean, I needed to pick up some things before I grab dinner. This way, I can give you a ride home since you're without Bessie for a bit longer." Micah shrugged and began to peruse the pancake mixes and syrups.

"I told you, I don't need a ride home," I bit out. Deciding I didn't want to play Micah's little game, I jerked my cart around and headed in the opposite direction.

I gathered the items of utmost importance, leaving any big or unnecessary items out until I had my car back. Rounding the corner toward the checkout, I saw Micah step up to the register one customer ahead of me.

Fuck my life.

"Really, giving you a lift is no problem at all." Micah spoke over the head of a mother and her two children between us.

I gritted my teeth and smiled as politely as possible. "No need. I'll manage just fine. It's not that far and I didn't get much."

The lady in front of me turned to look at my cart. "You can't carry all of that home. We take care of each other here in Blueridge Junction. You let Micah give you a ride."

"I'm good, honestly. I wouldn't want to inconvenience anyone." I wanted nothing more than to pay for my groceries and get the fuck out of the store.

"Nonsense." The lady clucked her tongue. "I'd be happy to give you a ride, but I've got the kids' car seats so no extra room."

A creaky voice from behind spoke up. "You'd be welcome in my car, but my three dogs are taking up the seats and they don't like to share."

I turned to see a decrepit gentleman and could only nod in acknowledgement of his statement.

"You really should let Micah give you a ride. He's a real dear. Always helping out and taking care of people in town." The middle-aged cashier nodded her head as she finished up Micah's order and started scanning the next items on the belt. "It would be downright silly and rude to turn down such a nice offer."

Micah gave me a shit-eating grin over the mother's head while she wrangled her groceries and children, and I fought not to climb over her cart and punch him. Or kiss him. Punch him, then kiss him.

I hoped that Micah leaving the store before I checked out meant that he'd given up on offering me a ride home.

No such luck.

When I walked out into the pleasant evening, there sat Micah's truck at the curb. And the man himself stood by the passenger door. "Throw your bags in the back." At least he didn't open the door for me. I fumed as I watched him walk to the driver's side. Was I angrier about the fact that Micah was pushing me or the fact that I found myself liking it?

"I'm starving. You okay with fast food?" Micah pulled the truck into a parking lot and headed toward the drive-through.

"I don't need anything," I groused feeling very much like a petulant child.

"It's dinner time, you gotta eat. What do you want?" Micah prodded.

"I'll eat at home."

"Suit yourself." Micah huffed then turned toward the speaker. "Yeah, I'll take two of your Big Meals, large fries and large Cokes with both of those, please."

Once Micah had paid for his food and turned his truck toward my crappy apartment, I was basically clamping my mouth shut to avoid drooling all over the interior of the truck. The damn food smelled so good. My cold cereal and toast wasn't going to compare. But at least we were almost to my place so I could escape the whole nightmare. I would have just sprang out of the vehicle as it slowed, but I had to get my groceries.

And Micah turned off the truck.

And gathered the food bags.

And climbed from the cab.

By the time I'd grabbed the leftover grocery bags from the back, Micah was standing at the stairs to my apartment door.

Fuck. My. Life.

"What the hell?" I growled as I shoved past him.

Micah reached for one of the grocery bags and gave me a cheeky smile. "I'm helping with your bags."

Deciding against making a public display on the sidewalk, I soldiered up the stairs. Unlocking the door, I blocked Micah as he attempted to bypass me.

"Thanks for the ride and carrying the bags. I can handle it from here."

"Shut up, Cole." Micah shouldered past me. "I'm not leaving until we've eaten this food and talked about some things."

Closing the door behind me, I leaned against it and stared, dumbfounded, at the man before me.

Micah Edwards.

Micah was in my apartment.

Fuck my life.

"If I eat and talk, will you leave?" I needed Micah as far from me as possible. He was too much of a distraction for my mind and body.

"Eventually." Micah tossed the fast food bags on the table and took a long slurp of his Coke.

I pinched the bridge of my nose. "We just talked a couple hours ago. Pretty sure we came to the conclusion that we agreed to disagree." I grabbed ketchup from the fridge.

Without even realizing what I was doing, I found myself sitting at the table with a burger and fries in front of me and Micah next to me.

"I had time to think. Some things have changed." Micah shoved some fries in his mouth, chewed then swallowed. "I think we can come to a better agreement."

Swallowing the bite of burger before it lodged in my throat, I could only stare. "What kind of agreement?"

"Eat your food. We'll talk in a bit." Micah smirked as if he knew the curiosity was killing me.

~*~*~

"Sorry, the place isn't much to look at." I hated the apartment, but it was all I could afford until I saved up some paychecks.

"It's fine. I'm not here to see your place, I'm here to see you." Micah followed me from the tiny kitchen in the corner of the studio apartment to the mattress I had placed against the wall.

"Someday, I plan to have some actual furniture, but for now I can offer you this lovely milk crate to sit on." I smiled ruefully at Micah. He took the crate, and I flopped down on the bed. "So talk." I was mentally and physically exhausted after going round and round with Micah.

"My parents have a shitty marriage." Micah settled on the crate as if preparing for a long story. "The only good relationship model I had as a child was Cody's parents."

I turned toward him. "Okay?"

"I want a good relationship. I want open, honest communication. I want my partner to be my best friend in love and in life." Micah ran a hand over his face. "Damn, I'm not making sense."

"Not really. I mean, that all sounds great. But maybe you should be talking to Cody about this. He's one of your best friends, he's out, so it would make sense that you two could make a go of it." I was truly confused where Micah was heading with this conversation.

He chuckled. "Cody is my best friend, but there's never been anything romantic between us. Maybe some sexual stuff when he and Levi and I were figuring things out at a younger age, but nothing more than that."

Propping up on my elbow, intrigued by the admission, I waited for him to continue.

"I'm willing to keep things hidden if it means a chance to get to know you better." Micah's words rushed out, surprising the two of us.

"What?" was all I could sputter.

Micah slid from the crate to his knees. "If you hadn't moved to BJ, we would have kept hooking up until one of us called it quits. No big deal. But having you move here seems like a sign that we could be something more and I.—"

"You want more than I can give you," I interrupted.

"Just hear me out." Micah reached for my hand. "Isn't there some quote about it being better to have loved and lost than to never have loved at all?"

"Quoting Tennyson? Impressive." I smirked although my heart was thumping wildly.

"I'm not saying we're in love. I'm not saying we're the perfect match." Micah's words came quickly as he stated his argument. "But, I think you're a great guy. The fact that we knew each other anonymously and then you ended up in the same small railroad town that I've lived in my whole life, it all just seems like too much to ignore."

"So, what are you saying?" I didn't dare allow my hopes to rise.

"I'm saying I'm willing to keep this thing between us hush-hush." Micah relented.

I narrowed my eyes. "For how long?"

The pain on Micah's face told me how difficult the decision was for him. "For as long as it takes. Maybe we find out we're not all that compatible and we move on as friends."

"And what if we find out we're perfect together?" The thought of a long-term relationship with Micah was more than I had ever allowed myself to dream of, but it wasn't something that could ever become a reality. I stared at him for a long time, letting wild thoughts run through my head. "What if I fall in love with you?" I whispered. "Things could get messy and ugly and we could get hurt."

"Let's just deal with things one day at a time, okay?" Micah rubbed a thumb over my hand.

"I have a feeling I'm going to look back on this day either with great joy or deep regret," I answered him honestly.

"So you're in?" Micah pulled me closer but stopped when his lips grazed mine.

"For now, yeah." The words were barely out of my mouth before Micah's kiss engulfed me and set my body on fire.

Tumbling us backward onto the mattress, Micah kissed me as if his life depended on it. "God, I've missed this. Missed you."

I pushed against his chest. "We can't have sex here. The walls are paper thin."

"Nothing noisy, just let me touch you and hold you." Micah pleaded.

I was helpless against him when he pulled the rubber band from my ponytail and ran his fingers through my hair.

"Gotta stay quiet," I murmured against his lips.

That was all the permission Micah needed. He jumped up to pull the shades on the two windows before stripping while standing in the middle of my tiny apartment. When I started to remove my clothing, he pounced on me. "Let me do that."

Relaxing back onto the bed, I allowed Micah to take over. With each piece of clothing he removed, I reveled in his whispers of approval and the kisses he feathered over my skin. By the time I was completely naked, my cock was achingly hard and begging for attention.

"Soon…," Micah licked his tongue around my nipple as he fondled my balls. "…soon I'll take us somewhere private where we can fuck each other's brains out." His promise made my cock jerk. "Mmmm, you like the sound of that, don't you?"

Micah knew I enjoyed him taking control and talking dirty. I threw my head back as his kisses moved up and teased against my neck. Spreading my legs, I welcomed Micah's hot and heavy body upon mine. Our dicks throbbed between our bellies and begged for thrusting friction.

I was lifted slightly as Micah snaked his arms under my back and hooked his hands over my shoulders in a tight hold. Cocooned by his heat, his scent, his hard body, I could only whimper as he began to rut his cock against mine. "Think about the next time we're together. My tongue will be so ready to eat your ass. I'll lube my fingers and loosen you up while I suck your balls. When you think you're going to die if I don't let you come, I'll line my dick up with your pretty hole and sink deep in your heat. You'll cry out my name as I rail your sweet ass, and you'll shoot all over your stomach as I fill you up."

Helpless against his words, my body tensed as his cock rubbed against mine over and over. I lost myself in Micah's kiss, groaning into his mouth as our release painted my stomach. Our dicks pulsed, sensitive and slick, in the mixture between our sated bodies.

After a quick clean up in the bathroom, Micah wrapped his arms around me, his front to my back, and walked us back to the mattress. "Tell me about you."

The question caught me off guard. We'd never talked much about personal information due to the whole anonymous thing. "What do you want to know?"

"What were you like as a kid? When did you know you were gay? What's your family like?"

"Whoa." I took a deep breath. "Diving straight in, huh?" I hadn't shared that much with anyone in my life for a very long time.

"If it's too much, just start small." Micah stretched out on his side, facing me, and stroked my arm.

"As a kid, I was a total spaz. All over the place. Probably annoying as hell. I was a jokester, always putting on a show. I was an only child, so my parents were a captive audience. I was spoiled in that I got all the camps and classes and clubs I wanted to join. My parents were both in education. My mom is still teaching, probably retiring soon if she can swing it. My dad was on the school board as president for several years." While things had turned sour as I got older, I couldn't help but smile as I thought of my younger days.

"I bet you were a cute kid." Micah traced my jaw.

"What about you?" I felt like taking the spotlight off me for a while.

"Hmmm, I think best way to describe me is, holy terror."

I laughed at Micah's description. "I can see that."

"My mom has always been milquetoast, so not only did she let my dad run all over her, she didn't do much to corral me." Micah smirked. "Dad was an ass from my earliest memories."

"Abusive?"

"No, not physically. But he never had anything nice to say. Everything my mom or I did was wrong. Even when we did things the way he demanded, he didn't like it and would find something wrong." Micah's memories turned his words bitter.

"How did you grow up to be so positive and good?" It amazed me that a kid could grow up the way Micah had and turn into such an obviously great guy.

"I don't know. I think it had a lot to do with Levi, Cody, and probably Cody's mom and dad too." Micah smiled. "Levi's parents were good people, but for some reason the three of us always gravitated to Cody's place and spent the majority of our time with his parents."

"What happened to Levi's parents?"

"They died in a car accident when we were in high school. After that, Hank and Marian were even more of parent figures for Levi and me." Micah shifted on the mattress. "I knew I was different than a lot of the guys at school in about fifth grade. They all started talking about girls wearing bras and short shorts, and I was more intrigued by guy's chests and their butts. Levi, Cody, and I never really talked about girls, but we also never talked about guys. We just hung out and watched movies and played video games and played on the hill. We were an inseparable trio from the very beginning. It wasn't until junior high that we figured out we were all gay."

"Did any of you think it was crazy coincidence that cousins and best friends would all end up gay?" I could just hear the people in a small town making comments about the three of them being gay.

"I think we were just so relieved to find someone else who liked guys, we didn't really even think about it. Until later. I mean, we joke now that it must be something in the water on Blueridge Hill. I've taunted my dad before with the fact that he may turn out gay if he keeps living on the hill." Micah laughed.

"So, did the three of you hook up?" I was curious and also partly turned on.

"Cody and I did. Levi and Cody did. Not Levi and me, that was just crossing the line in our minds. As we got older, we discovered other guys in town who were willing. Getting our drivers licenses was like opening a portal to freedom and sex. We could travel to nearby towns for hookups." Micah's brow furrowed. "I mean, I'm not a total slut."

"Hey, no worries. I mean, *we* met on a dating app. Neither of us is innocent." I trailed my hand down his arm and interlaced our fingers. "I felt different from my first memories, but I didn't admit I was gay until I was in college. I didn't admit it to anyone else until I graduated college. I was working at a small town high school in a neighboring town to where I grew up. Total hick town, but I liked the kids I was teaching." I sighed as the memories assaulted me. "I was naïve in thinking my sexuality wouldn't be a big deal. Maybe if I'd been a car salesman or a human resources rep or a banker, it wouldn't have mattered. But, the moment someone saw me out on a date with a guy, the nightmare started. I was harassed at school by a lot of the students. Some of them were supportive, but most were either scared of what they didn't know or just plain ignorant. The staff members were the same. Even the ones who tried to be supportive were pretty standoffish due to fear for their jobs."

"That's so wrong. It shouldn't happen like that. As a qualified teacher doing your job, your sexuality shouldn't matter." Micah barked out the words. "But, I know discrimination based on sexuality happens all the time."

"Well, I made the mistake of thinking my parents would be supportive. I went to them and explained what was going on. My mom was so-so. She said she was fine with me being gay, but told me I'd never be able to have a career if I was open about it. My dad blew up. I was a disgrace to the family name and our legacy in education. He loaned his power as a fellow schoolboard president to the board of my district and they forced me out. Dad said me leaving the school was for the best in the long run. Said it would give me the chance to start over. Fresh, new, and very definitely not *out*." Even after time had passed, I was still angry and hurt.

"When was this?" Micah's brow furrowed.

"Two years ago. I moved to Harriston, it's about an hour west of here and about the same size. I worked in a bank for two years. The hours were decent, pay wasn't bad. I licked my wounds and worked up my courage to return to teaching." Part of me wondered if I should have just stayed at that bank job.

"Why not get a teaching job in a big city?" Micah's question was one I asked myself a lot. "I mean, not that I'm upset about you ending up in BJ."

I smiled at his sweet words. "I'm a small town boy at heart. I don't feel at home in the city."

"But, can you really feel at home here if you can't be yourself?" Micah probed.

"Maybe this is the easier way. Maybe I'm just too scared to put myself out there in the big city." I shrugged.

"I'm not going to push you to out yourself, but I think you'd get a lot more support here in BJ than at your last school." He squeezed my hand.

"I'm a little traumatized by the last time, I really don't want to take that chance." In my heart, I wanted more than anything to be open and honest and just be the real me. But I couldn't open myself to the hurt again.

"Why teach? I mean, I know you're fabulous a teacher based on what Sadie says, but why not do a job that allows you to be who you really want?" Micah's voice was soft, not a trace of accusation.

"Teaching is in my family. It's what I'm good at. It's where my heart is. I feel alive when I'm in the classroom. When a kid finds a lesson fascinating or he finally *gets it*, it makes my heart soar." The thought of not having that in my life was overwhelmingly sad.

"What if you could have all that *and* be out?" Micah's eyes were hopeful, his words just a whisper.

"It would be a dream come true." I sighed.

"Dreams *can* come true." Micah ran a hand through my hair, cupping the back of my neck and pulling my face close to his.

"Dreams can also turn into nightmares," I murmured sadly.

With no answer to that, Micah grazed his lips over mine, softly at first then he deepened the kiss.

In return, I poured all of my dreams and wishes into that kiss, I worked to balance the longing of my heart and the bitter memories in my mind.

~*~*~

"As much as I'd love for you to stay." I stretched against Micah as we woke from a nap. "You need to go." It was dark out, and we'd been holed up in my place for much too long.

Micah's eyes were sad as he came awake beside me. "You want to come to my place?" His question was hopeful even as his face registered he knew what my answer would be.

"No. Secret means secret. We can't all of a sudden be seen with each other constantly." I hated it, but it was what I'd accepted my life to be.

"I can't and won't keep this from Levi and Cody." Micah's statement was firm.

"I'm okay with that. Please let them know the importance of keeping it quiet though. They're good guys, I know they would never out me on purpose." I didn't like the idea of more people knowing, but I couldn't deny Micah his best friends.

"And Jay has already guessed."

Micah's words didn't shock me. "Yeah, I figured that. He seems pretty perceptive for someone so young." I liked the kid, but his ability to see through me was unsettling.

"I think he seems younger than his almost twenty-one years. He *looks* so young, seriously the kid could pass for fifteen. But I think he reads people well." Micah rubbed his scruffy chin. "And I think he's going to be a handful for Levi."

"Jay and Levi?" Now, *those* words shocked me.

"I can't say for sure, but I think Jay is burrowing his way deep under Levi's skin. Levi won't act on it right now, but if and when he does, I think it's going to be explosive." Micah grinned.

"I'd hate to see Jay get hurt," I mused, thinking about the kid admitting he was a virgin.

"Levi would never hurt him. Levi's the type that once he makes a decision and acts on it, he's in it for the long haul. He's had tons of guys fall for him, but none have gotten to him. I think Jay may just be the one Levi can't fight." Micah shrugged as he stood from the bed and dressed.

"Can I see you this weekend?" I pulled my own clothes on.

"We can see each other as often as possible. I'll book a hotel nightly if that's what it takes." Micah's words seemed genuine, and I felt a twinge of guilt for making such a wonderful guy hide himself and bend to my ridiculous boundaries. But, selfishly, I wasn't going to look a gift horse in the mouth. I'd take what Micah was willing to give.

"Thank you for the ride home." I pulled Micah close and kissed him. "And for all the rest."

"No problem. I'm a good guy like that," Micah murmured in my ear before nibbling on the sensitive lobe. "But, I'll deny it if you start spreading rumors about me being too nice. I've got to keep my somewhat bad boy rep in place."

"You're the nicest bad boy I've ever met," I teased as I kissed his neck.

"Shhh, let's keep that a secret, too." Micah kissed me deeply and thoroughly before releasing me and walking out the door. I had a feeling watching him leave would get harder and harder each time.

CHAPTER 7

MICAH

"So Cole thinks you're willing to keep your relationship on the down low for an undetermined, possibly infinite amount of time?" Levi asked harshly.

"I may have let him think that," I mumbled before taking a sip of my beer. The three of us sat in Levi's basement. The one place we knew we wouldn't be bothered.

"But you don't really have any intention of keeping it secret for that long, right?" Cody's words held disbelief.

"No, the plan is that we will either get this thing out of our systems or it will turn into something more. I mean, I'm at least thinking it could turn into something more." I shrugged.

"And if it turns into something more and Cole holds fast to his decision to stay in the closet?" Levi huffed and shook his head in frustration. "Then you and he both get hurt. This is a stupid plan."

"Jay made it sound like a good plan." I pouted like a child, staring down at my beer.

"*Jay*?" Levi hissed. "You took love and relationship advice from a kid not even old enough to buy alcohol? Damn it all to hell, Micah. You and Cole deserve a chance if it's meant to be, but I'm not sure you're going about it in the right way."

"Well, this is me giving us that chance. If it ends up coming down to hard decisions, I'll fight for it, for whatever we may have between us." I drained my beer. "Who knows, maybe we'll end up getting bored with each other and drifting apart."

"I just hope you know what you're doing." Cody shook his head. "This could backfire in a bad way."

"Couldn't it also turn into something wonderful?" I felt like a sulky kid who wasn't getting his way.

"Yeah, it could," Cody agreed. "I just don't want to see you hurt."

"I gotta say, though," Levi interjected. "I've never seen you even close to this hung up on a guy before. He must be pretty special."

My heart soared. "He is." I felt my cheeks blush. "The attraction was immediate, but it's more than that. I can't explain the quick connection. It's like we've known each other our entire lives." I thought about something Hank had always told us. "You know how your dad always said he knew your mom was different from the moment he met her?"

Cody nodded and Levi followed suit.

"That's how I feel about Cole. It doesn't make sense, but it makes perfect sense." Was this whole plan going to be a complete bust?

"Well, that's clear as mud," Levi groused.

We spent the next hour shooting the shit and drinking beer. Having all three of us together with no one else around and no plans was a rarity anymore.

I did feel guilty leading Cole to believe we could work around his demands. But, holding him and talking to him felt so good, so I'd let things play out.

I couldn't let myself worry about the what if's. Cole was definitely worth the fight.

"We have the entire weekend?" Cole blushed as I started the truck.

Cole had driven to Levi's, parked his now repaired car in the garage, and I picked him up there. "Yep, tonight and Saturday night. We'll check out Sunday and then do whatever until we come back to town Sunday evening." I reached for his hand on the seat. "You get all your school work done?" I knew leaving on a Friday and being gone until Sunday would push Cole's paper grading time.

"Yep. The kids have a project to work on over the weekend, and I gave them a test on the computer so the grading was super easy." Cole smiled and squeezed my hand. "Thanks for this."

I glanced at him with a raised brow.

"Just…for the weekend and understanding where I stand." Cole shifted in his seat to turn toward me. "Very few guys like you would be willing to hide for me. I appreciate it."

"The hiding part sucks." At least I was being honest. "But, being with you is worth it." *For now* I added in my head. I wanted so badly to bring up that maybe we wouldn't have to hide forever, but I didn't want to put Cole on alert that I was already planning a non-secret future. *Damn, man, for someone so against hiding you've sure gotten it down to an art recently.* I cursed at the voice in my head and pushed the nagging guilt away.

Once we crossed the tracks and headed out of town, Cole slid to the middle of the seat and curled into my side. "So what are our plans this weekend?"

I smiled wickedly and waggled my brows. "Well, I thought we'd play some cards, maybe read a book or two, and take naps."

Cole laughed. "I'm all for the naps. Cards? How about strip poker?"

Rubbing my hand along his thigh, I squeezed lightly. "If I have my way, we will be so worn out from other activities that naps will be inevitable. And, honestly, I didn't make many plans other than sex and showers and food."

Cole tensed and moved away from me slightly. "Yeah, sex and food. That's about all we need, huh?"

I recognized the hurt in his voice immediately. "Hey, that's not what I meant." I put my arm around his shoulders and pulled him back to my side. "We will have weekends away where we go to movies, dinner out, shopping. But, with this being our first weekend together, I thought we'd keep it low-key and see how things work go. I wasn't sure how much time you'd want to spend in public, so I opted for more...private activities."

Cole relaxed and sighed. "This whole hiding thing isn't as easy as it seemed like it would be, is it?"

"I never thought hiding would be easy," I scoffed.

"I mean, when we're in BJ, we can go out together if the rest of the group is with us." Cole seemed to be thinking out loud.

"Which is still hiding, but it's like hiding in plain sight, ya know?" I followed his train of thought.

"Yeah." Cole slumped. "I mean, I want to think we can go out to dinner and movies and shopping on our weekends away. But, how would we ever explain it if someone from BJ saw us together?"

I wanted to scream in frustration over the whole situation, but instead I just gritted my teeth and hugged Cole tight. "Let's just enjoy this weekend. We can worry about the other stuff later."

Cole played with the radio until he found a station playing a wide variety of the biggest hits. Turning the volume down, he rested his head on my shoulder and kept his gaze on the highway before us. "Tell me more about Cody and Levi."

I smiled at the thought of my two best friends. "Levi is my cousin by blood. He's an only child. Rough on the outside, but has a heart of gold. Loyal, honest, and protective. Cody is not related by blood, but the three families have been friends and power players in Blueridge Junction for generations." I chuckled. "Well, as much as BJ can have *power players* these days. If that railroad ever goes out, the town would likely fade away. I think that's the biggest thing the Edwards, Wells, and Parker names stand for now in BJ, keeping the railroad going through town. It's basically the life source for most of the businesses."

"Is that a real threat? I mean, has the railroad said they could go elsewhere?" Cole sounded worried.

"Eh, every so often. There's another line that runs nearby. They could reroute the line that goes through BJ to the other line. But I don't know how serious the railroad is about it." I shrugged. I'd been hearing about the possibility of the railroad leaving town for as long as I'd been alive. "Since the trains stop, switch tracks, load, and unload in BJ, there are over a hundred people who would lose their job if the trains stopped coming through. Or, more accurately, they'd have to move out of town if they wanted to keep their jobs. That would take a lot of our population, our workforce, our consumers. Not sure the town could survive that."

After all the serious talk, we rode quietly for a few miles.

"So, you didn't finish about Cody." Cole broke the silence.

"Ah, Cody. He's the best. Truly. Hard worker, honest, loves with his whole heart. He loves running the B & B. He's really good at it, too. Comes naturally for him. He's a leader, always has been." I thought about all the times Cody had led our group into mischief.

"And Sadie is his little sister?"

"Yeah, she's more a sibling to me than my own brother. Mitch and I have never gotten along. But Sadie is a great kid. She came along when the guys and I were like twelve I think. So, she's basically had three big brothers growing up. She's a dreamer, a schemer, and a romantic at heart. Her goal in life is to see everyone she cares about happy." I let my head think a little deeper about Sadie. "Honestly, I don't know if she will stay in Blueridge. And I don't know if she should stay. I mean, she'll go off to college I'm sure, but my gut says she won't settle in BJ. I think she's got bigger dreams to tackle."

"Blueridge isn't a *bad* place to live," Cole protested. "I mean, I voluntarily came here to work."

"It's different when you're born and raised here." I frowned, trying to explain. "The guys and I all do work that can be done anywhere. We stay in BJ for our friendship, our heritage, and the fact that our jobs bring people from all around. I mean, Ed's Autos is known for fast, reliable, affordable service. It's why so many people from other towns bring their cars to us. I'm proud of that reputation, and I want to keep it that way. Levi's tattoos draw people in from as far as three hours away. He's built his business on amazing artwork, skilled inking abilities, reasonable prices, and reputable service. He couldn't stay in business if he relied only on the people of BJ. Even Cody gets a lot of boosted business from other towns." I slowed to take the exit from the highway. "But, Sadie seems bigger than Blueridge Junction. Maybe she'll prove me wrong, but I think she's going to take her talents somewhere else someday."

"Would you ever want to move somewhere else?" Cole lifted his head from my shoulder and rubbed at his neck as I pulled the truck onto a city street.

"Sometimes I think about it. But I wouldn't want to leave Cody and Levi. And I'd be just one of hundreds of mechanics in a bigger city. Big fish in a little pond seems safer than little fish in a big pond, ya know?" I glanced at Cole.

He nodded. "Yeah, I get it. Sort of the reason I don't see myself teaching in a big city. Small, rural schools don't have as much of the public eye on them. BJ's high school isn't making the news for failing test scores and having our staff and teaching abilities put under the microscope by the state to dissect each and every move we make." Cole smiled ruefully. "Plus, something about a small town just holds my heart."

"Is it how everyone knows your business?" I teased.

"Well, that part I could do without. I guess it's just the sense of community and belonging." Cole shrugged.

"So you feel like you belong in BJ now?" I arched a brow.

"I mean, I didn't at first. But, now, I have all of you as friends. I recognize people at the store and the B & B. Parents tell me how much their kids love my class. I'm getting great reviews when the administration does my observations at school. The students are learning and showing growth. So, yeah, I feel like part of the town." Cody nodded. "Maybe someday I can live in an actual house rather than that piece of shit apartment. I mean, I know I shouldn't complain, but having a crappy place to live is the one piece that's keeping me from feeling like I really belong. Pretty sure at least two of the other three tenants are strung out on meth at any moment in time. And the third may be a serial killer. He's got shifty eyes."

I laughed and pulled Cole close for a kiss. "You're amazing. I love how you make me laugh." My heart constricted as the word *love* flowed so easily from my mouth. I mean, I wasn't declaring my love for Cole, but as I mulled over the idea, I realized that *love* was very possibly exactly what I was feeling toward the man. But that was *waaay* too soon, right? Yeah, definitely.

"Where'd you go? You look like you're a million miles away," Cole whispered in my ear as we pulled up to the hotel.

"Nah, just got lost thinking about somewhere else you could live once you save up some money." It wasn't a lie exactly, I did think about Cole living elsewhere.

"Well, I don't have near enough money saved up right now, so the little shoebox hell-hole will have to do for now." Cole crinkled his nose.

"I made sure to get a room at the back so my truck wouldn't be seen from the road." I drove toward the back of the building. "I'll park here, walk up to get the key, and then we can unload." Leaning over to kiss Cole, I let my lips linger on his as I savored his sweet scent and soft lips. "I'm really glad this weekend worked out. No place I'd rather be for the next forty-eight hours."

"Me too," Cole murmured against my mouth before opening and taking my tongue deep. His arm came up around my neck then he kneaded his fingers through my hair before he whimpered against my mouth. Dropping his head back against the seat, Cole offered the seductive column of his neck.

Flicking my tongue over his Adam's apple, I licked at his skin and groaned at the distinctive flavor I'd come to know and desire.

Cole reached for my cock with one hand while palming himself with his other hand. "Oh God, Micah, you need to stop before I come all over my jeans."

His words permeated my foggy brain, and I pulled my lips from his slightly damp skin. "Fuck. Yeah, how about we take this inside, huh?" I chuckled and attempted to reposition my dick so I could actually walk. "I'll go get the key."

"You may want to get rid of that thing before you walk to the front desk." Cole flicked a hand toward my hard-on.

"Easier said than done. *Someone* got me all worked up and ready for more." I pulled him in for one last kiss.

"Think of dead puppies. Or going to the dentist. Or a really cold lubed glove during a prostate exam." Cole teased.

I shivered at the dentist and the cold lube. "Yep, there goes the boner. Thanks." I laughed and climbed from the truck. My cock was behaving itself for the time being. But I had plans for Cole that *definitely* didn't involve good behavior.

CHAPTER 8

COLE

Micah stalked back toward the truck and my heart caught when I realized the fire in his eyes was directed at me. He hoisted both bags from the back before grabbing me by the waist and lifting me from the passenger seat. Allowing my body to slide slowly down his front, I smiled wickedly as Micah moaned into my mouth. "Inside. Now. I've got plans for you." Micah bit at my lip as he spoke.

"Is this when we play cards?" I teased against Micah's mouth before biting down on his lip and swiping my tongue over any resulting sting.

"Yeah, I'm going to show you my club," Micah growled into my ear.

"You can be the ace in my hole." I chuckled at the rumble of laughter in Micah's chest and the hard thrust of his cock against mine. "Whoa, boy, no need to dig at me with your spade."

"Sorry, you've got me hard as a diamond here." Micah turned and pulled me toward the door.

"Sure hope you're ready to give me a full house," I murmured in his ear having way too much fun with the card analogy.

After unlocking our door, he pushed me inside and dropped the bags. Flipping on the light, he gave the room a cursory glance before putting the chain on the door and turning off the light. The room was washed in a soft glow from the natural light trying to get past the curtains.

"Get naked," Micah instructed as he began to strip.

Micah was sexy as hell all the time, but bossy alpha Micah was devastating. I shucked every piece of clothing and hurried to the bed. Spreading my arms and legs to enjoy the softness of the bedspread, I enjoyed the way my simple movements seemed to spur Micah on.

"I swear to God, Cole. Every time I see you, I think you can't get any sexier, and then you do."

Settling on the side of the bed, Micah then crawled on his knees until he knelt between my legs. He ran a warm hand down my chest, to my abdomen, and cupped my balls. "Look at you. You're beautiful, spread out on display for only me to see." He dropped to suck my cock. Wetting his finger alongside my length, he ran the slick digit to my ass and began to tease. "This is mine, no one else gets it."

I moaned as he swallowed my dick and breached my body with his finger.

"Say it, say no one else gets you." Micah spoke against the soft part of my belly, licking and nibbling.

"No one. Just you," I whined, writhing under him. "Please Micah, no more teasing."

He reached for his pants that had landed at the foot of the bed and pulled out a small packet of lube and a condom. Making quick work of the condom, he rolled it down his length never taking his eyes from mine.

I stroked my cock in anxious anticipation.

Waggling his brow, he shook the lube package and opened it. "Always be prepared." Micah poured the liquid into his hand. "Mmmm, it's warm from my pocket."

I groaned as he rubbed his slick hand up and down his shaft. Then Micah smeared the lube against my hole, and I gasped and rocked my body upward.

"Patience, baby." Micah murmured as he played with me first with one finger, then with two. "We'll get there."

"Not quickly enough. Come on, Micah," I pleaded.

"Playing the part of bossy bottom tonight will be Cole Pierce," Micah teased with his words as his fingers continued to tease my body.

"Shut. Up." I squeezed the base of my cock. "I'm going to come all over myself before we even get started if you don't stop talking."

"Now, whose fault would that be?" Micah batted away my hand and began stroking my dick. "I'm just being the caring partner and helping prepare your body for a hard and fast fucking. If you come before I even slide my cock deep in your ass, I'd say it's no one's fault but your own. You really should learn to control yourself, Cole."

I threw my head back and released a frustrated cry of longing.

"Okay, okay. I've got you babe, no more teasing. No more waiting. Put your legs on my shoulders." Micah helped lift my feet onto his shoulders as he lined himself. "Spread that sexy ass."

Opening myself to him, I pressed against his cock as it sank deeper and deeper into my body. The surging burn took my breath, but it was quickly replaced by the fiery fullness of having Micah completely inside me.

"Hands above your head," Micah demanded as he slowly thrust himself in and out.

Moving my shaky hands above my head, I felt my cock twitch when Micah pinned my wrists with one hand and gripped my length with his other.

Having Micah in total control of his body and mine was something I thought only existed in dreams.

"Fuck, baby. You're so good. So perfect." Micah chanted as he rocked into me over and over.

Moving so both of his hands held my wrists tight against the mattress, Micah increased the force of his thrusts, but slowed his speed. Pinned to the bed, legs folded up to my chest, I was completely at his mercy as he fucked me.

"Shit, Micah, please…," I begged.

Micah pulled from my body and hushed my protests as he ripped the condom off and jacked his steely cock in his hand until he was coming all over my chest. Leaning in to rub the ropes of white between our chests, Micah kissed me deeply and reached to stroke my dick. "Come for me, baby," he demanded against my mouth. "Cole." My name was a whispered prayer on his lips.

Crying out, my body shook as I lost myself to my release. Whimpering into Micah's mouth, I felt hot spurts explode onto my stomach. As I came down from my delirious high, I smiled sleepily when Micah mixed our spunk together.

"Are you drawing pictures in our jizz?" I asked, laughing even as he kissed me.

"Maybe." Micah drew something that felt very much like a heart in the stickiness on my stomach.

"Is that a heart?" My words were breathy, my heart pounding. It was crazy but sweet all at the same time.

"Had to stick with the card theme. Heart was the only one we hadn't used." Micah shrugged and kissed me soundly. He padded to the bathroom and then returned with a wet towel to clean up.

Micah stretched against me and groaned. "Mmmm, want to take a shower and then get some food?"

"Can I take a shower from bed?" My entire body had been given a workout, and I felt like I could sleep for days.

"Negative. Get that sexy ass of yours to the bathroom." Micah smacked my butt. "Just a shower, no extracurricular activity."

"Normally, I'd complain about that, but I'm not sure I have the strength to wash my hair let alone do anything more strenuous." I rolled from bed and stood up slowly. "I'm going to be sore tomorrow."

Micah waggled his brow and grinned wickedly. "You know, they say the best way to ease sore muscles is to use them."

"Who is they?" I laughed.

"They. The sex experts. The ones who know I need to ravish you again later." Micah sauntered to the bathroom and turned on the shower.

Climbing into the steamy shower felt amazing. The hot water on my skin, pelting my muscles, I could have stood under the spray for an hour. But, Micah's hands roamed up my back and traveled around to cup my chest, playing softly with my nipples.

"You said no extra activity," I whined.

"Nothing much, just want to hold you and touch you." Micah turned me around, pressing my back against the slick tile. "Maybe kiss you." His mouth touched mine, his tongue skimming against my lips.

We kissed for a long time. Just soft, leisurely kisses. Lazy kisses. Sated kisses.

Micah grabbed the soap. Rubbing it all over his body and building a lather in his own hands first before handing the bar to me. "Here, wash up." When we were both rinsed, Micah reached for the shampoo. "Let me do your hair."

I smiled and closed my eyes. Facing him without being able to see him, but feeling him so close was enough to bring some of my previously spent energy back.

"Keep your eyes closed, I don't want the shampoo to get in them." I could sense the focus in his words and feel his gentle effort against my head.

"I love your hair. I don't think I could have mine long, it would bug me and be in the way. But yours is beautiful. Love to have it in my hands." Micah scrubbed my head and walked me backward under the spray to rinse the lather from my hair. He used some of the leftover bubbles and ran his hands through his own short hair. "Mine's easier, too."

By the time we were out of the shower, dried, and dressed, I was feeling a little more pep in my step. "Want to go grab food or have something delivered?" I flipped a paper over on the desk and read the list of local restaurants and delivery options.

"Order in and watch a movie?" Micah raised his brow.

"Sounds good. You pick the food and movie," I suggested.

"You should pick something, this is your weekend, too."

"I'll pick food and activity tomorrow. Promise." I flopped onto the bed, smiling at Micah as he scanned the paper.

The next thing I knew, Micah was shaking me awake. "Hey, babe. Food's here."

I sat up on the bed feeling groggy. "Shit, I'm sorry, I didn't mean to fall asleep. How long was I out?"

"Only about forty-five minutes. I let you sleep until the food got here. But now it's time to eat and I've got a comedy movie queued up on the TV." Micah pointed to the food displayed on the tiny desk.

"Mmmm, how did you know I love breakfast food for dinner?" I grabbed one of the Styrofoam containers and inhaled deeply. Pancakes, bacon, sausage, and eggs. Reaching for a fork, I noticed another package. "Are those biscuits and gravy?"

"Yep. Local restaurant serves breakfast all day and offers delivery to this place. Figured it was as good if not better than pizza or something." Micah shrugged and spooned some biscuits and gravy into my makeshift bowl of deliciousness.

"This is almost as good as sex." I groaned around a bite of pancakes. "This all looks homemade.

We need to have Cody offer a standard breakfast meal available for purchase all day long. People would flock to get food like this in BJ."

"If this breakfast food is almost as good as sex, we're clearly doing it wrong." Micah's eyes twinkled as he watched me over a forkful of food.

Taking our food to the bed, we settled in to finish our dinner and start the movie.

Two hours later, we were still full from pigging out, and our cheeks ached from laughing so hard at the movie. With only the bathroom light giving a slight glow to the room, Micah clicked off the television and pulled the covers back. He kissed me softly before reaching to strip my shirt over my head. I removed his in return. We shucked our shorts and cuddled under the blankets in the chilly hotel room.

"I love the heaviness of hotel blankets. Love to set the room super cold and then snuggle under the covers." I shivered as I spoke, but felt the comforting heat of Micah's body as he pulled me close.

"What else do you love?" Micah whispered.

You. The word was right on the tip of my tongue. But no way would I say it. Not yet. But…it felt so right in such a strange way. Loving Micah shouldn't feel right, but in that moment, the emotion seemed natural.

Instead of letting my crazy heart do the talking, I started listing things I loved. "Mmmm, naps are great. Breaks from school are nice. Love the change in seasons, especially fall and spring. Accomplishing a goal. Seeing my students grasp a concept. New socks. Cats." I paused in my list to catch Micah smiling at me as I spoke. "What?"

"That's a very broad list you've got there." He kissed me on the nose.

"What about you? What do you love?" I wanted to know everything about the man.

Micah stared at me for a long moment before he finally cleared his throat and spoke. "Um, I love rainstorms. Love to sit out on the porch and watch the lightning. I like to take things apart and put them back together, fix things. And laughing with my friends." He traced a finger down my arm. "Now, what about things you *don't* like? Pet peeve type stuff."

I thought about his question. "I get aggravated when people walk *in* the *out* door or the other way around." I paused. "People who drive slow in the left lane. Being late. And rude people. What about you?"

"I'm on board with all the things you listed. Also hate when people are having loud conversations on their cell phones in public places like we all want to hear what they are talking about. And when parents don't keep an eye on their kids. I mean, I've had parents totally oblivious in the shop and next thing I know their kid is standing next to me."

"Oh, tell me about it. How about the parents who think their kid does no wrong?" I rolled my eyes. "Like it's my fault that I've had the kids studying for a test for three weeks, and I've sent at least five messages and study guides, but then the kid gets less than an A and the parent is like, 'But, he didn't even know there was going to be a test.'"

"Well, I guess you probably would have liked my parents if I was a student in your class. Dad would have never believed me over a teacher and most definitely wouldn't have stood up for me." Micah shook his head.

"No, that's not what I mean." I reached for his hand, trying to soothe him. "Parents should *always* be on their kids' sides, but I think parenting is about finding that happy-medium between indulging kids and handing them everything and being their best friend versus allowing them to learn from their mistakes, accept consequences, and support them but keep them accountable."

"Yeah, my parents were definitely neither of those types." Micah frowned. "I think that's why I work so hard to be a better person. I want to treat people right."

"Do you ever think you'll have kids?" The question was out of my mouth before I even knew what I was saying. "I-I mean...someday, with...ah...with the right person."

Micah caught my chin and brought my mouth to his. "You're adorable when you get all flustered." He kissed me. "Yes, I definitely want kids someday. With the right person." He winked. "What about you?"

"Yeah, I think so. I mean, I know parenting is a fucking hard, full-time job, but I think I could be a good parent. But I wouldn't do it just to prove I can, ya know?" I took advantage of being close to Micah's lips and leaned in to nibble them.

"What do you mean?" Micah questioned.

"Just, I see a lot of people having kids or adopting kids and using them as a status symbol or to make themselves look good or as a big middle finger to those in society who say certain people shouldn't be allowed to have them." I shrugged. "If the right person and I decide someday to have kids, I want it to be because we've thought it through and we know we have the love and support to give to a child. I don't want my kid to just be for show."

"I'd never really thought of it that way, but you're right." Micah laid his head down on the pillow and pulled me to his chest. "I see people sometimes who act like they don't even like their kids. It seems unfair to the couples out there who want a baby so badly, either naturally or through adoption, but some people mistreat their children like they wish they'd never been born."

"Yeah, and so many kids out there need a good home, but couples who don't fit the mold aren't considered acceptable parents." I spoke softly against his chest, loving the sound of his slow breathing and the thump of his heart against my ear. I loved that Micah and I could go from silly and taunting, to sexy and sensual, to casual and relaxed and never miss a beat.

The steady rhythm of our hearts and our breaths lulled me into a peaceful sleep.

CHAPTER 9

MICAH

"You snore." Cole whispered in my ear.

"Do not," I grumbled, but smiled as I turned to pull him into my arms.

"It's okay, it's sort of cute." Cole buried his head in my chest.

"Mmmm, you're cute. But I don't snore." I held him for several minutes as we dozed off and on. When he shifted his legs and I felt his hard length against my thigh, I chuckled. "Well, good morning to you. Ready for round two?"

"That sounds lovely, but I'm seriously so sore, I don't think I could take you again," Cole muttered as he continued to snuggle against me.

I was silent for a moment. "What if I took you?"

"No, really, last night was great. But my ass is sore and I probably won't walk right for days." Cole laughed.

"I mean, what if I bottomed?" My cock immediately took interest in the idea.

"Really?" Cole propped up on his elbow. "Do you even like to?"

I pretended to think it over, tapping my chin. "Hmmm, do I like having a deliciously sexy man fuck my ass? Well, I don't know. I should probably take a few days to think it over."

"Don't be an ass." Cole punched my arm. "I just mean, you never seemed to want to switch."

"That's because railing your ass is something fantasies are made of." I kissed him. "Doesn't mean I am against having you fuck me." I pulled back to look at him. "Unless you're just not into it."

Cole tapped his chin, mocking me. "Hmmm, do I want to drill a deliciously sexy man's ass? Well, I don't know. I should probably take a few days to think it over."

"Shut it." I pulled him on top of me, hoping the mix of our morning breath canceled each other out. "And fuck me."

I didn't have to tell him twice. Cole dove head first off the bed to grab his bag. Ripping out a condom, he had it rolled down his swollen, hard cock before he even made it back to the bed. "Please tell me you have more lube."

"Nah, between your finger, tongue, and spit, we'll be fine." I winked.

Cole blanched slightly. "I don't want to hurt you."

"You seriously think I came all this way carrying only one little packet of lube?" I rolled my eyes and pointed toward my duffle. "Side pocket."

Cole grabbed/found it and slicked himself and his hand before generously coating my ass. "It's, um, been a really long time since I've done this. I might not be any good." He worried his bottom lip between his teeth as his finger teased my hole.

"Fuck that. Everything we do is perfect. Now, finger me." I spread my legs and tried to relax against the burning stretch as Cole worked my body open.

Stroking my dick, I let my muscles accommodate Cole's fingers.

"How do you want to do it?" Cole whispered, kissing along my jawline and onto my neck as he continued to work me.

"On our sides is good." I turned to my side and waited until Cole was spooned up behind me. Positioning my top leg over his hip, I cupped my balls as Cole directed his cock to my hole.

Reaching around my shoulders, Cole pulled me close and nibbled my ear as his body took mine.

The pain was breathtaking, but Cole's murmurs against my cheek helped to ease the discomfort.

"God, baby, it's never been this good." Cole's words seemed to catch in his throat, sounding as if emotion obstructed them.

With each and every long, slow stroke into my body, Cole's impressive length touched upon that magic spot. Within moments, I felt my balls draw up. "I'm gonna come, Cole. Fuck." I shot my release and threw back my head, offering Cole my neck to bite and lick.

"Fuck, yeah." Cole continued a slow and steady rhythm for several minutes until his body tensed and he thrust hard and deep. His cock pulsed as my body milked him.

We laid together in a sweaty, sticky twist of arms and legs until we caught our breaths.

"Shit. That was amazing." I held Cole's hand against my chest.

"Beyond amazing," Cole agreed.

As we lay tangled together, my heart thumped with a realization. No matter if it seemed too quick, I was in love with Cole Pierce. "Can I tell you something and you promise it won't ruin the rest of our weekend?" Blood rushed through my veins and my heart pounded in my ears.

"Nothing you say could ruin this weekend," Cole whispered.

I turned to face him, cocking my head in disbelief. "Pretty sure I could say some things that would ruin a weekend. But hopefully this won't be one of them."

"Go for it." Cole's sexy hooded eyes watched my mouth, waiting for my words.

"I know it's crazy, but I think I'm in love with you." The words rushed out of my mouth, and I never wanted to take them back.

Cole's eyes immediately sparkled with tears. "You think or you know?" His words came across as a hopeful whisper.

I pulled him close, cupping my hand around the back of his neck. "I *know*. I started falling for you the moment we met, and I've been falling hard ever since. I know it's fast and I know it's crazy and I know we have issues to work around, but, it's the truth. I love you." I dropped my mouth to his and kissed him deeply. When Cole pulled away, I worried for one split second he hadn't liked my confession. "Hey, don't cry. I didn't mean to make you sad." My heart nearly stopped as I thumbed away his tears.

"Don't be stupid. These aren't sad tears. These are happy, *I love you, too* tears." Cole's words tumbled out before he kissed me until I was dizzy. "I've never felt this way about anyone. Ever. I don't care how fast it happened. I don't care how crazy it seems. I don't care that we've got some issues to work around. I love you." He laughed and sobbed and sniffled against my shoulder. "Sorry, I'm getting you all snotty."

"We're laying in last night and this morning's sexed up sheets. Pretty sure a little snot is the least of my worries." I hugged him close.

We laughed together then rested in happy silence for a long moment.

"Hey, so when Cody closes BJ's each Sunday, he's not really having church is he?" Cole's errant question made me laugh. My plan was seemingly working, we'd gotten all lovey dovey, and Cole goes all random with a question about the B & B. I smiled and hugged him tightly.

"No. Well, not church in the way you're probably thinking." I didn't want to reveal too much to Cole, but I knew Cody was always open about that part of his life if someone was truly interested. "A group of people meet there regularly. So, in that way, it's like church. But maybe *club* or *meeting* would be a better description."

"Is it like AA?" Cole's concern was genuine.

"No, Cody isn't an addict or alcoholic. He gets his highs from other things."

"Do you go to his club meetings?" Cole reached for my hand.

"I've been. I like the people there. It's not really my scene, but I support Cody."

"So, what is it? He's not like doing something illegal is he?" Confusion clouded Cole's face.

"No, babe. Nothing illegal. In fact, Kennedy usually attends a lot of the meetings." I had to chuckle at the thought of Cody and Kennedy. The men acted as if they hated the other, but anyone with two eyes could see they were crazy about each other.

"Cody and the rest of the group are into the leather scene. Lots of slings, floggers, ball gags, cock rings, nipple clamps."

Cole's eyes widened. "Whoa, that was *not* where I saw that going." He tilted his head. "That's cool. I could totally see Cody and Kennedy doing that. What about Levi?"

"Nah, you're more likely to find him at a strip club than at a leather club." My mind wandered briefly to Levi watching a certain young twink dancer we all knew. That relationship had tropes written all over it, but I could see it working if Levi would ever just give in.

"Maybe Cody would let us come to a meeting sometime?" Cole appeared intrigued.

"Sure, I know he wouldn't mind." I shrugged. Suddenly, the thought of introducing Cole to the leather scene, even if just on the periphery, seemed like a fabulous idea.

Conversation turned to what we'd do for the rest of the day. "We could go to that outlet mall," I suggested.

Cole tapped his bottom lip. "No, too much risk of a student or parent being there."

For a brief moment, I felt the room closing in on me. It was as if I was suffocating in the secrets and hiding. Hadn't expressing our love for each other changed anything between us?

But, watching Cole light up when he talked about the movie he wanted to rent and the food he was going to pick for the day, I shoved the worry away. What Cole and I were finding with each other was worth it. Right?

"Okay. Let's shower." I smacked Cole's ass. "Then we can grab food. Let's get something for a couple meals. That way, we can stay in bed naked all day."

"Sounds like the perfect plan." Cole smiled as he strolled toward the bathroom. "You know, I could get *really* used to weekend getaways like this."

Walking into the bathroom, I grabbed Cole by the waist and swung him around to the sink. "You know, we can do these weekends in BJ just the same." I savored the way Cole's legs immediately opened to make room for my hips, pulling me close, and locking behind my thighs.

"Maybe once in a while, if we can figure out a way to get me to your place without anyone else knowing." Cole worried his lip and met my gaze. "This doesn't change anything. I love you, but I can't go through the pain and hardship that being gay brought me at the last school."

I fought against frustration that bubbled through me. Sighing heavily, I whispered, "I know. And I'd never want you to have to go through that. I think most of BJ would react in a different way if they ever found out. You're an amazing teacher and most of the town loves you."

"It's not the part of the town that loves me I'm worried about. It's the small percentage who don't like me, will never like me, and who will look for any reason to boot my ass to the curb." Cole's brow furrowed. "People like that are vocal and can turn a town against a person."

Like my dad. The thought was in my head before I even saw it coming. "Maybe someday it can be different." I let the conversation go because we had the rest of our weekend together and we wouldn't be making any huge decisions right then anyway. "Come on, we're wasting hot water."

The rest of our weekend was spent eating sub sandwiches and copious amounts of Chinese, watching an action movie and a horror movie, and making out in bed.

By the time Sunday morning rolled around, I was feeling torn about the day. One part of me wanted to laze around in bed with Cole for another day or two. But the other part was getting a little stir-crazy being cooped up in the room. I wanted fresh air, sunshine, and walking down the sidewalk with Cole's hand in mine. Would we ever be at that point? Even with our confessions of love something in my gut told me prying Cole from his closet was going to be harder than I had originally thought. If only he could see BJ the way I saw it. Yeah, some people were hateful and mean, but the town was fairly accepting or at least looked the other way. Him being out wouldn't be perfect, but I couldn't see the school getting rid of him over his sexuality. I hated that he had such a crappy experience tainting his memories.

I heard Cole's phone buzzing from somewhere on the floor. "You gonna get that?"

Cole snuggled closer to me, "Nah. It can wait. I just want a few more minutes with you."

When my phone immediately started ringing, I got a bad feeling. Rolling to grab the phone from the bedside table, I saw Kennedy Marks was calling me.

"Morning, Kennedy. What can I do ya for?" I knew my voice sounded scratchy and sleepy. I knew Kennedy was obviously/likely well aware that Cole and I were together. And, deep down, I knew something was wrong. Kennedy didn't usually make Sunday morning calls just to chit chat.

"You got Pierce with you?" Kennedy's question was hushed.

"Yeah, I do." I sat up. Looking down at Cole, I noted his sleep-rumpled hair, his pink, swollen lips, and his pretty blue eyes staring up at me. I reached for his hand knowing something bad was coming.

"Good. Keep him with you. He's going to need you. But you probably better head back to BJ." Kennedy's words were clipped. "Put him on the phone."

CHAPTER 10

COLE

Micah's face was full of concern when he thrust the phone at me. "Kennedy wants to talk to you."

My eyes bugged and my first thought was to refuse the call. But I trusted Kennedy just like I trusted Cody, Levi, and Jay. Assuming Cody had told Kennedy where I was, I took the phone and croaked out a rough sounding, "Good morning."

"Cole, Micah's going to drive you back to Blueridge Junction. There's been a fire at your building." Kennedy's words were calm and to the point, but I could hear the regret in them. "I'm sorry, man."

"The whole building or just my apartment?" Either way was bad, but if it was just my part of the complex, it immediately sent my thoughts racing to someone wanting to hurt only me.

"Whole building. Investigators are looking into it. Looks like one of the apartments had a meth lab. Blew up and caught the whole damn place on fire." Kennedy's voice became muffled as he spoke to someone in the background. "Listen, just get on back to BJ. We can talk more then. Put Micah back on the phone."

I numbly handed the phone to Micah and flopped back down on the pillow.

"Was anyone hurt?" Micah's words registered, but were far off as I listened to him talk. A few minutes later, Micah ended the call and then gathered me in his arms.

"I'm sorry, babe." His kiss to the top of my head was as comforting as his warm hug. "Let's clean up real quick and get back on the road."

"What did he say?" I shivered with chill and fear of what the answer would be.

"About what?" Micah rubbed my arm.

"Was anyone hurt?" The thought of anyone getting hurt soured my stomach.

"No. No one was home in any of the four apartments. No injuries, just material loss." Micah stood and pulled me from the bed. "Come on, let's get going."

Hot showers and brushed teeth were all we took time for.

"We'll grab coffee and breakfast on the way home." Micah put his arm around me and pulled me close, kissing the side of my head. "I'm so damn glad you were with me."

The catch in his voice and the sniffle of his nose brought my own tears. Turning in his embrace, I buried my head against his shoulder. "I have nothing now. Nowhere to go, no clothes other than the ones I have on. Fuck, Micah, what am I going to do?"

"Shhh, we'll figure it all out," Micah whispered. "And don't you ever say you've got nothing. You've got the fuckin' BJ boys on your side and there ain't nothing better than that."

Micah's attempt to cheer me up brought the slightest of smiles to my face. "Thank God for the BJ boys." I wiped my nose and grabbed my bag. "Okay, let's go see what the damage is."

I nibbled at the breakfast Micah bought. The coffee might have tasted good, but I was too lost in thought to enjoy it. I ate and drank only because I knew Micah expected it and because I'd need something in my stomach to face my destroyed apartment.

The fact that we arrived at the scene together, in Micah's truck, floated somewhere in the back of my mind, but I pushed it away as I saw the charred remains of the building I'd once lived in. Strange how I had hated the place, but felt betrayed and hurt and lost to see the shell of my former home smoldering on the corner lot.

"I knew they were some meth heads, but I didn't realize they had a meth lab in their place," I murmured as Micah squeezed my hand before we got out of the truck.

"Hey, I love you. You've got this, we'll get through it." In order to keep up the façade to the public, Micah pretended to look at the fire's destruction, but he was speaking to me. "If I could, I'd take you in my arms right now and kiss you."

I played as if I was looking at the remains of my home, as well, but responded to Micah's words. "Thanks. I love you, too. I'll take you up on that kiss a little later."

Acting as if we were just two buddies, Micah and I climbed from his truck and walked toward the fire scene. Kennedy met us, shaking both our hands.

"Sorry to have to call you with news like this." Kennedy's words were soft and his face grim. "You can't go in right now, too hot and too dangerous. If the firemen or investigators find anything salvageable, they will pull it out. But I'm guessing not much survived." Kennedy put a comforting hand on my shoulder. "Where will you be staying?"

The question was like a punch to the gut.

Where *would* I be staying?

"Mr. Sutton made it clear that me staying at the school was a temporary situation." I began running through the scarce options in my head. "I'll probably have to get a hotel room while I look for rent options."

"I'll let you know where he's staying," Micah cut in, breaking into my thoughts. "You need him for anything else?"

"No, I'll contact you if we need anything else. If there's a bright side to this it's that your car wasn't here. The vehicles would have likely been destroyed, as well." Kennedy clapped me on the back and then pulled Micah into a hug. "Take care of him." I heard Kennedy whisper to Micah. The fact that Kennedy knew Micah would be the one to comfort me proved Cody and Kennedy were probably closer than some of us had first thought.

"Always," Micah replied before turning to me. "Let's go. There's nothing you can do here."

We were back to the truck and driving up Blueridge Hill before my head/surroundings came back to me. "Where are we going?"

"Well, your car is at Levi's. Thought we'd get it and then figure out your living situation." Micah reached for my hand, offering an anchor in the ocean of emotions.

When we arrived, Cody and Levi were on the porch waiting for us.

"Did you tell them we were coming here?" I glanced at Micah.

"No." Micah smiled ruefully. "We know each other so well, they probably just knew to expect me. I'm guessing word of the fire spread pretty quickly through BJ."

My heart warmed at the thought of having friends and family know me and love me that much. "Must be nice to have that."

"It is. And you have it, too. I'm here for you. Levi and Cody are, too. Kennedy didn't *have* to track you down. Hell, I half expect Jay to arrive sometime today." Micah pulled his truck into the garage and shut the door.

"Yeah, but Jay would use any excuse to come see Levi." I tried humor, but my words fell flat.

Micah pulled me across the truck seat and wrapped his arms around me. "True. But he'd come to help you whether Levi was around or not." Cupping the back of my head, Micah dropped his lips onto mine. My body lit on fire as his tongue and lips poured love into that kiss. My world outside of the truck was a mess, but in a cozy little space with Micah, I could attempt to forget the chaos.

Slowing the kiss, seeming as reluctant to end the moment as I was, Micah pulled away. "Damn, I love you so fucking much. I'm so sorry about the fire."

We held each other for several more minutes. "Cody and Levi probably wonder what happened to us." I drew in a deep breath to fortify myself. "I better get going." Reaching for the door handle, I felt Micah grab my arm.

"Get going where?"

"Looking for rooms and places to rent," I snipped. Guilt immediately gnawed at me. My stress wasn't Micah's fault.

"We'll figure it out here, together." Micah's words were a command leaving very little room to argue.

"As much as I'd like that, I can't just hang out here indefinitely. It's bad enough that we were seen riding into town together and then leaving town together. I need to keep my distance." My heart hurt. I wanted to stay and let my new friends help me. But, my fear and anxiety insisted that sticking around with these guys would be dangerous to my career.

"Fuck that. Come on." Micah jumped from the truck and trotted around to my door before I could even make sense of what was happening. He yanked open the door and pulled me to my feet. "We'll get it all settled. We're your friends. It would look more suspicious if we *weren't* helping you. This isn't about gay or straight, this is about friends helping friends."

When we reached the porch, Jay had indeed shown up. "You kids get in some good garage sex?" The kid was beautiful, endearing, and irritating beyond belief.

"Knock it off, Jay." Levi growled.

"Sorry, Daddy. I'll be good." Jay teased and batted his lashes while he trailed a finger over Levi's broad, inked shoulders.

Levi dropped his head into both hands and groaned.

Jay smiled broadly from behind Levi's back.

Cody just snickered.

"Thanks for being here." Micah addressed the men I was slowly beginning to realize were actually my friends too. "Cole's will need a place to stay. While I'd be more than willing to let him move in with me," Micah cast a look my way and my heart dropped to my knees, "I'm guessing he's not on board with that plan."

My face must have shown my extreme terror at the thought of moving in with Micah because he wrapped an arm around my shoulders and pulled me close. "It's okay. Too much going on right now to worry about that. We've got all the time in the world, but let's figure out where you *are* willing to stay."

"It's not that I *don't* want to live with you." I knew my words were iced in panic and the guilt surged once again.

"I know, I know, it's that you *can't*." Micah kissed the side of my head. "For now." When he winked at me I wasn't sure if it was meant to tease or comfort.

Micah turned back to the group. "The next best thing would be the loft above the shop. It's not in the best of shape, but we could get it fixed up."

Levi grunted. "Yeah, about that. I already spoke to dear old Uncle Ed about Cole using the loft. He said no."

"The fuck he did," Micah growled.

"It's okay. I'll find someplace." I didn't want Micah upset with his father because of me.

Micah ignored me and yanked his phone from his pocket. He walked to the edge of the porch and stood with his back to us. Four pairs of eyes glanced around uneasily, all of us knew the conversation was not going to go well.

"Here I thought I'd saved him from this lovely experience by talking to Ed already." Levi rolled his eyes.

"Dad? So, the new teacher in town, Mr. Pierce, needs a place to stay. His place burned down. I was thinking we could show some good ol' Blueridge Junction hospitality and let him stay in the loft above the shop." Micah was doing a nice job of keeping his voice calm and not projecting the hostility he'd displayed just moments earlier.

Maybe Ed Edwards was speaking extra loudly or maybe it was because the four of us were waiting in an uncomfortable silence, but we could hear his words plain as day.

"Better take yourself down a notch or two, boy. I'm the owner of the shop. Don't go making any decisions about *my* business or *my* building. I already offered the loft to one of the other fire victims." Ed's smug words hung in the air.

"You'd risk having a meth head living above the shop before allowing my friend to stay there?"

Micah's voice was rising. I watched his shoulders hunch and his hand move up to his face. No doubt pinching the bridge of his nose in frustration.

"I'd rather have a *real* man staying in *my* building than some pansy-ass sissy boy." Ed shouted. "This right here is why you ain't ever gettin' your hands on my business. Over my dead body!" The air was silent, only the echo of Ed's words reverberating around us.

"Well, that went well," Jay muttered.

"That mother fuckin' piece of shit," Micah roared.

I walked to him and wrapped my arms around him, pulling his back tight against my front. "Shhh, it's okay. Don't let him get to you. He's not worth it."

Micah spun around. "But *you're* worth it. I hate him and his bullying, hateful ways." Sighing loudly, he looked over my shoulder. "So, what's the next option?"

"I'd be happy to have you stay with me," Jay piped up. "But, it's a studio with a twin bed and not much else. You're welcome to stay for a day or so until we figure something out."

I smiled at the kid. "Thanks, Jay."

Jay shrugged as he placed delicate hands on Levi's shoulders. "I mean, you're not my *type*, but we could be snuggle buddies for a few days."

"Lay off, Jay," Levi growled and stood as if fleeing from Jay's touch. He paced the porch for a moment before stopping and addressing the group. "How dumb can we be?"

"Huh?" Cody's question spoke for us all.

"I've got a perfectly good guest house here on the property. Cole can use the house for as long as he needs. Permanently actually." Levi gestured toward the back of the property with a strong, inked-up arm.

"Oh my god, that's perfect." Jay clapped. "I can come visit and spend time with my Daddy, my Papa Bear, and my Papi. Maybe we can have a sleepover!" Jay sauntered toward me, his hips swishing gracefully as he stalked me like prey. "Hmmmm, what should I call you? Padre? No." Jay tapped his chin and studied me a moment longer. "Professor? Yes! It fits you."

"I'm a social studies teacher, far from a professor." I laughed and blushed at Jay's ridiculous nickname.

"Nope, Professor it is." Jay smiled triumphantly.

"Can we get back to the issue at hand?" Levi groused.

"Oh, Daddy, I'll take your issue in hand anytime." Jay threw the words over his shoulder.

Levi threw his hands up. "I give up. I'm opening up the guest house if anyone wants to come with me. Jay, you're welcome to make like a tree and leave."

Micah knocked Levi in the back of the head, but Levi kept walking.

"I'd *climb* you like a tree, Daddy." Jay's saucy response almost hid his frown after being dismissed.

"Aargh!" Levi groaned and disappeared around the back of the house.

"Why do you mess with him so much?" Cody grabbed Jay in a headlock and ruffled his hair. "I mean, don't stop doing it, I love seeing him so flustered. I just have never seen someone get to him the way you do."

"What can I say?" Jay shrugged as he ran fingers through his messy hair. "Natural talent."

As the three of them headed down the porch steps to follow Levi, Micah turned to me. "Coming?"

I walked with the group, unsure of the plan they seemed to have laid out without any input from me.

The guesthouse was gorgeous and at least four times bigger than my little apartment. For a brief moment, I imagined myself living there. A real kitchen, a full size refrigerator, an actual bed instead of a mattress on the floor. The house was still completely furnished from when Levi had lived there. I'd have real furniture, a stove rather than a hot plate, and a bathtub instead of a tiny shower stall.

"Levi," I started, my voice shaky as I knew I had to turn down the offer. "This place is absolutely beautiful."

"Yeah, it really is nice. Sometimes I think I should've stayed here instead of moving to the big house." Levi checked faucets and light switches as we wandered through the house.

"I can't stay here," I blurted.

Four pairs of eyes pinned me to the wall. Jay looked confused, Levi looked affronted, Cody looked shocked, and Micah looked sad—which hit me the hardest.

"Why?" Jay asked.

"The rent would be way higher than what I was paying. Living on Blueridge Hill with three of the town's hottest gay men would definitely call attention to me. And I can't rely on you guys to rescue me." My heart hurt as I spoke. Damn stupid past experiences constantly controlled my life.

"Fuck that. You're staying here, end of story." Micah jabbed my chest with his finger. "You need a place to stay. I need you safe. Levi didn't even ask you for rent, so don't assume he'd charge you an exorbitant amount to stay here. No one is going to question you living on Blueridge Hill."

I rolled my eyes, partly touched that Micah obviously cared so much and partly pissed off that he was all up in my shit.

"Okay, fine," Micah huffed. "Maybe a few people will question it. But, your place just burned down. We're your friends. It makes complete sense for us to help you find a place to stay." Micah's eyes seemed to plead with me to change my mind.

"Honestly, it would be more questionable if we *didn't* help you out with a place to stay." Cody interjected. "I mean, can you imagine the talk around town if you ended up sleeping in your car while Levi has a perfectly good house for you to use?"

I wanted to stay strong, but the emotions of the day and their arguments were getting to me. I took a deep breath, suddenly feeling tired and beyond overwhelmed.

Micah stepped close enough I could feel the heat of his body against mine. "Baby, please. Do this. For me. I'm keeping a secret for you. At least do this so I'll know you're safe and comfortable." He leaned in, resting his forehead against mine. "Please?"

My heart broke into a thousand pieces then soared higher than ever before. Micah's words, his pleas, his love shattered me. I could no more tell him no than I could stop the sun from rising.

With tears pooling in the corners of my eyes, I cupped the back of Micah's neck and pulled him in for a kiss. "Okay. I'll stay. For you." I murmured against his mouth.

"For both of us." Micah kissed me back. "I love you so damn much."

"Ahem." Levi cleared his throat. "While this is beautiful and touching…"

"And fuckin' hot as hell," Jay quipped. "Admit it, Daddy, you'd like to back me against a wall all dominant and then turn all soft and sweet and caring before you kissed me into oblivion."

"Shut up, Jay," Levi growled. "As I was saying, this is great, but can we move things along. You guys can use the bedroom a little later."

Micah and I broke apart. "Sorry." I sniffled.

"In terms of rent, I don't expect any—".

"But," I interrupted.

Levi pinned me with a glare. "That being said, *if* it would make you feel better, you can pay rent in the amount you were paying at the other place."

Micah stiffened. "Now, wait a minute."

I laid a hand on Micah's chest. "No, that's perfect. Thank you so much, Levi." Turning to Micah, I smiled. "I won't be a leech. Let me pay something. It's the only way I can even begin to make this okay in my mind."

"Fine. As long as I know you're safe and comfortable, I'll deal with my cousin making you *pay* for a place to stay later." Micah turned a disgruntled glance toward Levi.

"Hey, man, back off." Levi held up his hands. "I got him to stay, that's what counts." "Yay! So, it's settled!" Jay bounced on his feet. "I think we should plan a big *welcome to your new place* party! How about tomorrow night? We all bring a dish and we'll hang out here. Cody, you can bring Kennedy."

"Why the fuck would I *bring* Kennedy Marks anywhere? You want him here, *you* invite him." Cody frowned at Jay. "But, I'll bring food from the B & B."

"Guys, I don't even have clothes, I think a party may be a little premature," I argued.

"No worries, you can do your part by making sure the house is clean. We'll take care of the food and drinks. And we'll gather you some clothes." Jay popped his hip out. "Don't worry, Professor, we got you." Jay winked before turning to Levi. "As much as I'd love to stay and play, Daddy, I'm heading out so I can get ready for the party. I work tonight."

"So?" Levi snapped.

"So, just thought you might like to come watch the show," Jay purred.

"I'll pass, but thanks." Levi shook his head.

"Afraid you won't be able to fight it once you see me all decked out and dancing on stage? The invitation is open. Come watch anytime." Jay brushed a kiss across Levi's cheek before sauntering toward his car. He flashed us a grin and flicked a quick wave before he got in his vehicle and headed down the hill.

"Dude, you are so fucked," Cody taunted.

"Shut up," Levi growled.

In the end, Micah stayed to help me clean up and prepare for the party. Cody and Levi both went to work.

I started the day homeless and ended the day with an actual home. The fact that Micah had been by my side, an unwavering strength the entire day, made my heart swell with love and affection. Maybe

Blueridge Junction was where I'd truly be able to settle in and make a life.

CHAPTER 11

MICAH

"Where you goin'?" My dad demanded from the front porch as I rounded the main house to hop in my truck the next evening.

Taking a deep breath, I realized I was more than ready to have it out with my dad and this was as good as time as any. "I'm heading over to Levi's. He was kind enough to let Cole Pierce stay in the guest house. We're having a little house warming party."

"Damn faggots," Dad muttered under his breath.

Taking the porch steps two at a time, I quickly found myself towering over my dad as he peered up at me with hate-filled eyes. "You wanna say that again, old man?" Something about having Cole in my life sparked my anger toward my father and lit a flame to stand up to him more than I ever had before.

Dad pushed himself from his chair. "Said you're all a bunch a damn queer-ass homos. Bringing a bad reputation to Blueridge Junction and smearin' good family names."

"Don't you ever get tired of beating this horse, Dad?" I took a slight step backward, thinking that possibly Dad and I could have a decent discussion. "Yes, Levi, Cody, and I are gay. That's not changing. We're not the only gay people in town. We won't be the last gay people in BJ. Maybe spend less time focused on being angry and just accept it and let it go. I'm not saying approve of it, just stop letting it eat away at you. Spend some time with Mom, show her some of the Ed Edwards she fell in love with."

"Getting knocked up don't constitute fallin' in love you damn idiot. You keep associating with the likes of them and you'll find yourself out of work in addition to not owning the business." Dad put his hands on his hips as if his words were a triumphant jab.

I took another deep breath, determined to keep myself as calm as possible. Running a hand over my face, I thought my words through for a moment before speaking. "You know, *Ed*, you've been using that threat for a mite too long. Don't want me to take over the business? Fine. Have it your way. Give the shop to Mitch. I'll start my own shop. I have the money saved up. I have the reputation to pull it off. I have the business mind, and you know damn well I have the mechanic skills to run Mitch out of business. In fact, I look forward to it."

Dad's face boiled in anger. "Ed's Autos has been a part of this family and this town for generations. You wouldn't dare see that legacy fail."

"Watch me." I winked, feeling damn fantastic that I'd finally recognized that Dad's threat didn't affect me any longer. "Now, I'm heading to Levi's to spend the evening with my friends."

"You better watch yourself, boy. You like having a place to live? Better remember that." Dad blustered to the point of spittle flying from his mouth.

"Dad, I could not care less about living in the guest house. If having me there is a problem, let me know. I can be packed and out of your hair within a day." The thought of moving out actually sounded damn good.

"Where the hell you think you'd go? No one in BJ wants a damn homo living with them." Dad's words were meant to hurt, but they simply rolled right off.

"I'll stay with Levi, stay with Cody, hell, I even bet I could stay with Kennedy. Not everyone in this town is an ignorant, weak homophobic asshole." I turned and marched down the steps. It felt good to finally tell my father where he could shove himself.

As I backed my truck from the drive, I felt the angry heat of Dad's gaze following me. I owned my truck, I had money saved up, and I could set up my own shop and run circles around Dad if it came down to it. I smiled triumphantly; things were going to be okay.

I smiled as the gang brought in tray after tray of food. I knew the BJ boys would come through.

"Oh my gosh, guys," Cole gushed in amazement. "This is way too much. Look at all this food! What am I going to do with all of it?"

"Well, I for one, plan to *eat* a lot of it," Jay crowed as he helped himself to a slider, a pickle spear, chips, and a cookie. "Anything you don't want, send with me. I am the queen of the doggy bag."

"We'll split it up." Cole smiled.

"Oh! I almost forgot. I have a package for you." Jay's eyes lit up and he rushed outside to his car while Cody, Levi, Cole, and I could only stare after the kid.

When Jay returned, his arms were full of a large basket wrapped up in a bow, and Kennedy Marks was walking behind him.

"I went out to grab the package and came back with two." Jay sat the basket down and turned toward

Kennedy. "Something tells me *this* package would be a lot more fun to play with though."

I laughed. "Down, Jay. Down, boy." Reaching for Kennedy's hand, I welcomed him and dodged daggers being shot at me from Cody. "Good to see you, man."

"Thanks for the invite." Kennedy shook my hand with a good-natured smile.

"*You* invited him?" Cody hissed at my ear when Kennedy turned to talk to Jay.

"No, *I* invited him." Levi smiled wickedly at our best friend. "Figured if I have to put up with Jay, you can deal with having Kennedy here."

Hoping to change the subject before the two pulled out their fists, I nodded toward the basket. "Jay, what's in the basket?"

"I don't know. Someone in town gave it to me and said to make sure I got it to Cole." Jay shrugged.

"Well, you better open it." I smiled at Cole.

Cole blushed, but dropped to his knees to pull the gigantic bow from the oversized basket. Lifting layers of tissue paper, Cole uncovered several stacks of clothing. "Oh my gosh," he whispered.

"Whoa! Looks like someone just hit the fashion jackpot." Jay clapped his hands.

"This is way too much. Who gave this to you?" Cole demanded.

"A true lady never tells her secrets." Jay made a display of locking his lips and throwing away the key. "But, I think there's a note."

Cole pulled an envelope from inside the basket and opened it. Scanning the card his eyes immediately began to sparkle with building tears. "It's too much," he choked out.

I walked closer and pulled Cole to his feet. "What's it say?" I wrapped him in my arms. Cole handed me the card, and I read it aloud.

"*Dear Mr. Pierce,*

We are sorry about the fire at your apartment. We took up a donation throughout town and used the money to buy you some new clothes. Figured you'd need them for school mostly.

Your Friends in Blueridge Junction"

"Awww, that's too sweet," Jay gushed. "Now, go try them on!"

"Come on. We'll take the basket to your room. You can go through things *later*." I spoke to Cole but gave Jay a pointed look.

"Okay, fine. You can try things on later." Jay pouted. "But I want to see what you got."

Cole and I reached his bedroom and I had barely placed the basket on his bed when he threw himself into my arms and sobbed.

"Baby, what's wrong?" I ran my hands up and down his back. Cole cried for several moments before he pulled his red, splotchy face away from my chest.

"I'm sorry, seems like all I do is cry and snot on you." He reached for a tissue to clean up his face. "I can't accept those clothes."

"Of course you can. It's small-town hospitality at its best. Friends and neighbors pitching in to help where help is needed." I thumbed a stray tear from his cheek. Maybe Cole would see all the hiding and secrecy was no longer needed. Would seeing how much people care about him make him realize the town wouldn't care if he came out?

"It feels like I'm getting preferential treatment. You think anyone delivered a basket of clothes to the other victims?" Cole's words held guilt.

"Two of the victims left town to live with family for the time being. The other is living above Ed's Autos. Did any of those three people ever go out of their way to be friendly or helpful or even slightly pleasant to the folks of BJ?" My brow furrowed. "No, they didn't." I didn't wait on Cole to answer. "Don't you worry about them. There are resources in town and outside of town to help them if they need it. If it makes you feel better, I'll personally make sure the guy living above the shop has the information for those resources." Using my knuckle to tip Cole's chin, I looked him in the eye. "You're one of us now, you're part of this town. Let folks help in the way they know best. One day, you'll be able to pay it forward."

Cole took a deep shuttering breath. "I just haven't had anyone do something so nice for me in such a long time, it's hard to imagine that it was really meant for me."

"Just accept the gift, say thank you, and be grateful. Your biggest need aside from a house was clothing and now you're set with clothes, too. Write a thank you note if you'd like, Jay can take it back to the anonymous donors." I pulled Cole in for a tight hug. "You ready to go back out there and enjoy your party?"

Cole smiled and nodded. "Yeah, let's go." As we walked from the room, Cole jerked on my arm to stop me. "Hey, we need to make sure Jay takes home a good amount of this food. I get the feeling he doesn't always eat as well as he should."

My heart swelled to the point of bursting, and I kissed the top of Cole's head. "You got it. We'll make sure he gets his share."

~*~*~

When I got home that night, my dad practically gave me a heart attack.

"Damn it, old man, what the hell you doing in my house?" I grabbed my chest and attempted to slow my breathing and calm my racing heart. When I'd turned on the kitchen light, I'd nearly pissed my pants to see my father sitting at my kitchen table.

He held a bottle of whiskey in one hand and a gun in the other. "Hmmm, which would be better? Kill the pansy with a bullet or shoot him where it hurts most and kill his career?"

Dad sing-songed his slurred words.

My heart caught in my throat. "What the fuck are you talking about?" I heard the quiver in my voice but hoped Dad didn't.

"I got the scoop on Mr. Teacher. Got kicked out of his old school and town for being a cocksucker." Dad chuckled and took another swig of the whiskey. "Shooting him in the head would be quick, but messy. Making trouble for him at school would take longer, and probably be just as messy, but a lot more entertaining. Don't ya think?"

My dad was drunk and he had clearly lost his mind.

"Just let it be, Dad. Cole isn't hurting you or anyone else." I tried to keep my voice calm.

"Ain't gonna just 'let it be' when that cocksucker is running my family name in the mud." Dad waved the gun around his head.

"Dad, with or without Cole in town, I'm gay. Always have been and always will be." I could only hope my words were making their way past the booze. But, the way Dad's eyes glazed over, I had my doubts.

"No. Before he showed up, you at least took your dirty queer ass out of town. Don't think I didn't know where you were going and what you were doing. Makes me sick. But I let it go because it wasn't taking place in BJ." Dad shook his head, his lip curling into a sneer. "But, now, you're running around with that pansy and people will start to talk."

"Talk about *what*, Dad? I'm gay. I'll tell anyone who asks, I'm gay. It wasn't a secret before Cole came to town."

"But now you go flaunting it around like it's some kind of proud thing. Ain't nobody wants to see that queer shit right in their own town, right in their own face." The more Dad chugged whiskey the more agitated he became.

"Dad, there's a gay bar at the edge of town. Plenty of folks head there to watch guys dance. Hell, Cody closes down the bar every week and more than a couple residents take part in that event. People in BJ don't really care, why should you?" I felt my frustration level begin to rise.

"Maybe it's about time someone did care about that shit!" Dad roared and pushed himself up from the chair, knocking it to the ground. He was out the door within seconds, but I was left standing in complete and utter shock.

Grabbing a bag and throwing the essentials into it, I rushed to my truck. I made it to Levi's in record time. Bounding up the stairs, I pounded on his door.

"What the fuck, Micah?" Levi answered the door in just his boxers.

"My dad was sitting in my kitchen, in the dark, drinking and waving a gun around. He threatened to either shoot Cole or ruin his career." The words rushed from my mouth as I tried to catch my breath.

"Go, get out to the house. You can stay as long as needed." Levi motioned me toward the guest house. "Tomorrow, we'll talk to Kennedy. I doubt there's anything that can be done about drunken threats, but we need Kennedy to help us convince Cole that you need to stay with him."

"Fuck, he's not going to like this. I'm either protecting him from a bullet to the head and all but flushing his job down the toilet, or I keep my distance to help his job and take the risk of my dad acting on the threat to shoot him. What the fuck do I do?" I pleaded with my cousin for an answer.

"Right now, just go to Cole. Explain what happened. Offer to sleep on the couch if need be. But you have to keep him out of harm's way." Levi nudged me toward Cole's house.

CHAPTER 12

COLE

The pounding on the door set my senses on alert immediately. Staying in a new place as someone's guest already had me on edge. Having people start making assumptions about either Levi and me or Micah and me had me extra edgy. But the loud thumping on the door sent me over the cliff.

Pulling on a zip-up hoodie in a pathetic manner of protection in addition to the new velvety soft sweatpants I'd donned after a shower, I shuffled my socked feet to the hallway and peeked around the corner. I wasn't sure who or what I expected to see at the door. But Micah wasn't it. The sight of him brought a quick smile to my face. But, when I saw his grim expression through the door's window, I knew he hadn't come back this late just to visit. Plus, hadn't we discussed not hanging out together without the other guys?

I got to the door just as Micah turned to scan the darkness beyond the house. Yanking the door open, I started to speak, but Micah pushed me inside. "Shhhh. Don't say anything. Go to the guest room."

Micah rushed me past the room I'd claimed as my own and shoved me gently inside the smaller dimly lit guest room. When he threw a black duffle bag on the floor and squatted to the floor to hold his head in his hands, I worried. "Micah, what's wrong?"

"Just give me a second," he panted. Running large, shaky hands through his hair, Micah breathed deeply. Collapsing to his ass, he jerked his shoes from his feet and tossed them to the corner.

"Micah, you can't stay here. You know that. What's with the bag?" I hated not being able to let him stay, but having him at my house when it was just the two of us would look suspicious.

"I have to stay. I know you don't want me to, but it's for your own safety." Micah's words were rushed and still breathless. He had obviously gotten to Levi's in a hurry.

"My safety is the issue if you *stay*."

"No, look, I need to call Kennedy and tell him what happened. He'll tell you the same thing I'm telling you." Micah reached for my hand and pulled me to the floor with him. Jerking with a start, he jumped to his feet. "Hang on. I'll be back. I need to pull the blinds and check the locks."

When he rushed from the room, I felt more spooked than ever, but I was getting frustrated with not knowing what was going on. I followed Micah down the hall. "Babe, I really…"

Micah turned on me. "No. Get back in the room. At least until I check the house and talk to Kennedy. I'll tell you what's going on, but I need you to stay out of sight for now."

Stubbornness is a strong suit for me, so I stood in the hallway outside of the guest room with my arms crossed, frowning, until Micah came back.

"Really? I'm here trying to save your ass and you can't even follow a simple direction?" Micah smirked at my belligerence as he pushed me back inside the guest room. Backing me up to the bed, he only stopped when my legs hit the mattress. Wrapping his arms around me, Micah pulled me tight against his chest. "Damn it, baby, I love you so much and I'm so sorry."

"Sorry about what?" Were my words as exasperated as I felt? *Good.*

"When I got home, my dad was sitting at my kitchen. In the pitch black. Well into a bottle of whiskey and wavin' a gun around." Micah held me close and rocked me from side to side.

"Oh my god, what the hell? That's crazy."

"Yeah, it scared the shit out of me, but then he started talking shit about killing you or your career. We went a couple rounds over me being gay, you, the shop, and then he left. I know he was drunk, but he was definitely threatening you. You can't stay here alone."

The meaning of Micah's words hit me. My stomach churned at the thought of Ed Edwards making good on either of his threats against me. But my anxiety rocketed at the thought of Micah staying in the guest house with me. "Micah, you can't stay here. It would just make it worse for both of us." My words said one thing, but the fear in my heart wanted to beg Micah to stay. Ed Edwards was a scary man.

Pulling his phone from his pocket, Micah punched Kennedy's number as he positioned us comfortably on the bed. "Kennedy." Micah paused. "Yeah, I figured he'd call you. So, what do you think?" He listened to whatever Kennedy was saying. "Okay, yeah, that will work. Yeah. Thanks, man."

Handing the phone to me, Micah smiled apologetically. "He wants to speak to you."

"I feel like speaking to you is starting to be associated with bad news," I huffed into the phone.

Kennedy's rough chuckle held no humor. "Sorry, Cole. Listen, I think Edwards was likely just spewing shit through the whiskey, but I'd rather not take any chances. I'll visit the shop tomorrow and talk to him, see if I can get a feel for whether he was serious or just blowin' smoke. But, until then, I think you better let Micah stay. Have him park his truck in Levi's garage. You guys lay low and let me see what I can find out."

"What about work? We both have jobs." No way could I take off days from school at this point.

"Go to work as usual. I'd just rather Micah be there at least tonight. Plus, you know neither of you would sleep a wink if you were apart knowing about Ed's threats." Kennedy's voice held a smile and it irritated me that he spoke the truth.

Sighing deeply, I pinched the bridge of my nose. "Okay. Thanks. Let me know what you find out." I ended the call before tossing the phone to the side. "Well, this is just great. Fuck. My. Life."

"Baby, I'm sorry. I knew my dad was a prick, but I wasn't prepared for him to turn psycho." Micah pulled me into his arms and held me tight as his voice rumbled into my hair. "Please, I know this isn't the way you wanted things to be, but I can't stand the thought of you getting hurt because of my dad. I'll sleep on the couch or in the guest room if that helps. But, please, don't push me away right now."

The tears that caught in Micah's throat did me in. Taking a shuddering breath, I relented. "Fine. You can stay." I turned to kiss him. "You're right, I definitely did not *want* my apartment to burn down, my boyfriend's father to threaten my job and my life, and to likely be outed because of it, but I need you to know and understand one thing."

"What?" Micah pulled back, his brow furrowed as he watched my face.

"No way in hell are you sleeping anywhere but in my bed tonight. You can't come in here and tell me your father wants to kill me and then bunk on the couch. It's just not proper." I winked and kissed him again.

Micah chuckled. "Okay, okay. I understand." He kissed me deeply, his lips and tongue conveying his sorrow for the situation and his love for me. "But, I think we should sleep in the basement or something. My dad knows the layout of the house, he'd know which windows to break if he wanted. The basement would provide more protection."

"That's fine. The basement it is." I rolled from the bed. "Let me grab some things to take down there."

"Okay, but don't turn on the lights." Micah gathered his shoes and bag and waited for me in the hallway, his gaze scanning the house like a watchman.

When we got to the basement, I realized we could live down here for at least a week. "There's a full bathroom and bedroom and living room down here?" I gawked around the spacious area.

"Yeah, kitchenette too. Nice little bachelor pad if ever I've seen one." Micah tossed his bag and shoes to the floor again. Walking from between the small block windows to check they were all shut and locked. "We can get ready for work down here in the morning."

"Speaking of the morning, my alarm is going to go off at the butt-crack of dawn. If I don't get some sleep, those kids will murder me tomorrow." I yawned and stretched my hands over my head.

Micah winced at my choice of words.

"Oops, sorry. I guess it's better the kids metaphorically murder me in class than your dad murder me for real in my bed." I shrugged, feeling punch drunk with the mixture of exhaustion, emotion, anxiety, and fear.

"Not funny," Micah admonished.

By the time Micah had pulled down the covers, I was swaying on my feet. "Come on, babe. Time for sleep." He pushed me gently to the mattress and climbed in beside me. "Take this off, I want to feel you against me," Micah whispered in my ear as he slowly trailed the zipper of my hoodie down. Shrugging from the jacket, I relished the warmth of Micah's chest against my back and his strong arms around my body.

My heart caught in my chest. How could I love this man so very much and yet deprive the two of us of the simple act of sleeping in the same bed? Tears began to flow.

"Shhhh, babe, what's wrong? I'm so sorry." Micah rolled me to face him.

"I'm just thinking that we won't ever get to have this. Us, here, together. The secrets and hiding will always keep us from just a simple night of sleep in our home." My words were groggy, my head fuzzy, and my heart in pain.

"Shhhh, it's okay. I love you, you love me. Let's just get through this for now." Micah kissed the top of my head.

I swore I heard him whisper, "Never say never" as I drifted to sleep.

The hard length of Micah's hot cock pressed firmly against my thigh. My body and my dick both woke instantly. "Mmmm, good morning," I groaned.

"Roll to your back," Micah demanded, his morning voice gruff and sexy.

"We have to go to work." I managed a slight protest, but rolled to my back.

Spreading my legs, Micah trailed kisses along the inside of my thighs before licking and sucking my balls. "I want to wake up with you beside me every damn day," Micah murmured before taking my cock in his mouth.

"Micah." My gasp was of pleasure and protest.

"And I'll take you any damn way I can get you." Micah moved to nestle his hips between my legs and whispered against my mouth while his cock rocked against mine. "If that means hiding, or moving, or fighting, I'll do it. I love you, Cole. So damn much it hurts."

Lost in a wave of emotion and pleasure, I swiped at the tears on my cheeks before wiping tears from Micah's face as well. I held our throbbing cocks in my tear-stained hand and pumped them in a slow and steady rhythm. "I love you, Micah. With everything I have."

Our releases mixed with our tears as we continued to rub our sensitive shafts together.

"I mean it, Cole. I will do everything in my power to make sure we can have mornings like this." Micah kissed me.

"Sometimes wishes and dreams are outside of our control." I whispered sadly against his lips. "Come on, we're going to be late if we don't get ready."

People at school looked at me strangely.

They gawked, giggled, whispered.

Or maybe I was being paranoid.

Within the first hour of school, I felt like I'd developed a nervous twitch. Every chuckle, every cough, every word took on a new meaning. Were they directed at me? Shit, the whole thing with Ed

Edwards had messed with my head more than I originally thought.

"Nice shirt, Mr. Pierce," Sadie winked as she walked past my desk to leave class.

"What's that supposed to mean?" I snapped without meaning to.

Sadie frowned. "Um, just that I like the shirt. You okay?"

I ran a hand over my face. "Shit, I'm sorry. The fire and some other crap have me a bit off kilter. Thank you for the compliment."

Sadie's mouth formed a grim line. "I'm sorry about the fire. And, maybe I wasn't supposed to find out, but I'm really sorry about Micah's dad being an asshole. I overhead Cody talking to Mom and Dad."

Worry rushed through me. There was absolutely no way to keep a secret in a town like Blueridge Junction. The majority of the gossip wasn't meant to hurt or harm, but keeping folks from talking was hard. Ed Edwards had one of the most efficient grapevines in the world at his disposal if he chose to use it.

"It's okay. Just a lot to deal with." I smiled at the girl. "Hey, speaking of the shirt, do you happen to know who was responsible for the generous clothing donation?" I cocked a brow at Sadie.

Her cheeks pinked and she smiled. "Gee, Mr. Pierce, I don't know. I mean, quite a few students and other people in town really like you and are glad to have you in BJ. I'm sure anyone could have facilitated a quick donation collection and headed to the closest mall to buy new clothes sure to make a favorite teacher look stylish even during a crappy time."

I narrowed my eyes and studied Sadie's face. "Mmmhm. Well, I'm not sure *anyone* could have done it, but I hope that person and those who pitched in know how very much the gesture meant. It was truly appreciated."

"Oh, I'm sure they know. If I ever hear who it was, I'll be sure to pass your message along." Sadie winked.

"You do that." I chuckled and then watched the girl head toward her next class.

I plodded through the next three periods on autopilot. My head wasn't into teaching, but the students didn't mind extra time to work on their projects. The whispers and giggles were definitely present, but perhaps I was making more of them than necessary. I mean, high school kids whispered and joked and laughed all the time, but I couldn't get the worry and fear out of my head. My brain and heart were at constant odds as I contemplated the best way to move forward.

By the time lunchtime rolled around, I had formulated a plan I didn't even realize I'd been considering. My subconscious had been hard at work. I had absolutely zero idea of what I was going to say or do, but I knew I had to confront him. Would my plan do any good? Or would it cause more trouble than it was worth?

Only one way to find out.

I headed toward Ed's Autos.

CHAPTER 13

MICAH

"Is Ed in?" a voice asked from near the shop door.

Holy hell. Cole.

I glanced toward the office where Kennedy had just left from a little chat with my father before turning my attention back to Cole. Wiping my hands on a rag, I moved slightly closer to him before I spoke. "He's here. But I don't think he's in the greatest of moods."

Cole cocked his head and smirked. "Is he ever in a great mood?"

"Good point." I chuckled. "But, still maybe not a great idea to be here." I really didn't want to set my dad off. He'd laughed with Kennedy and said his threats had been "all in good fun." But I didn't trust him.

"Listen, I've got lunch and prep period before my next class. I don't have a ton of time." Cole caught my eye and spoke seriously. "I need to do this, Micah."

"Fine. Leave the door open so I can hear what's going on. And I *will* jump in if he gets rough or violent, to hell with the hiding and secrets." My heart was pounding a mile a minute with anticipation and pride for Cole. If he was willing to stand up to my dad, maybe he was willing to open himself to being who he really was.

Cole walked straight into my father's office without knocking. I stood as still as a scarecrow, holding my breath, as the scene played out before my very eyes.

"Mr. Edwards, I was hoping I could steal a little bit of your time." Cole held out his hand which Ed stared at with a curled lip but didn't shake.

"What the hell are you doing here, boy? I think you've already stolen enough from me." Dad sneered. "You've got my son, what else do you want?"

"Micah is a good friend, yes, just as many other people in town have been." Cole's words flowed from his mouth, but I had a feeling he had absolutely no clue what he was going to say until he heard the words himself.

"*Friend.* Right," Dad scoffed. "I don't got much time, so get on with it."

I was shocked Dad was allowing Cole to speak. Maybe his drunken threats had been just that, or maybe he was trying to toe the line after his visit from Kennedy. Either way, I waited anxiously to hear what Cole had come to say.

"Mr. Edwards. I'm a good teacher. I'm a good citizen. Many people at the school and in BJ like me and respect me." Cole's words were solid and held no trace of the sheer panic I knew had to be coursing through him. "I let hateful bullies run me out of town once before, but I won't let it happen this time. I've started to feel like BJ is my home, and I don't have any plans on leaving."

Ed threw his head back and laughed an evil laugh. "Oh, that's rich. Did this pansy ass faggot just come here to threaten me? Stand up to me? Well, challenge accepted. We'll see how tough you're feeling when the whole town learns you suck cock."

"Sir, at no time have I brought my sexuality into this conversation." Cole's voice wobbled slightly.

"Ahh, so you're admitting you're a homo?" Dad taunted.

"I'm asking you to back off and leave my job and me alone. I'm telling you I won't be run off." Cole lifted his chin.

"Well, ain't the little faggot cute going all butch on me." Dad stood from his chair behind his desk. "Don't tell me what you *won't* do, boy. I'll have you out of town before you and your little boyfriend even know what hit you. Now, get out of my office." Dad pointed toward the door.

Cole stared at Ed for a brief moment and then nodded his head in silent acknowledgement.

As Cole walked past me, I grabbed his elbow and rushed him to the side door where we'd have a little privacy. "Cole, baby, that was amazing, but what did you just do?" I kissed his lips, his eyes, his chin, his nose.

Cole laughed through tears. "Probably just signed my own resignation and death certificate."

"Why did you come over here?"

"Your dad was going to be a thorn in my side no matter what. He'll be even worse now, but I took it all laying down last time, and I refuse to just roll over this time." Cole's face registered pride and fear. "But, oh fuck, what the hell did I just do?"

I laughed and kissed him again. "Well, I think you just laid down a challenge to Ed Edwards and promised him he could bring his worst."

Cole ran a hand over his face. "What the fuck was I thinking?"

Pulling him close to me, I rubbed his back. "I think, just maybe, that you were thinking you love your job, you love Blueridge Junction, and you love your friends. You were forced away from all of that last time, but you're older and wiser now and I think your heart and head just worked together to take a stand." Kissing his ear, I couldn't contain my smile. "And, now, no more hiding."

Cole jerked back from me as if I'd bit him. "What do you mean? Of course there's hiding. Even more so now."

"You basically just outed yourself to my dad and admitted we were together." My heart hurt and my head was trying to catch up to what Cole was saying.

"No, I asked your dad to back off and told him I wouldn't be run out of town. I said nothing about being in love with or involved with you and nothing about being gay." Cole stepped farther away, his hands on his hips.

"So, wait. You're willing to stand up to my dad to save your job, but you're not willing to admit you're with me?" I wasn't sure if I was angry or hurt. *A little of both.*

"If I were to admit I'm gay, the handful of people against me would have even more ammunition to get me out of town. Right now, they have their assumptions and rumors and hearsay. If I lose this job, I won't be in BJ any longer anyway." Cole's words were making absolutely no sense. "You said this morning you'd do anything to keep me. Do you still mean that?"

"I said I'd do anything in my power for more mornings like the one we shared." I protested, frustrated he was using my words against me.

"Well, if you want to keep me, I need you to be willing to keep things hidden. Plain and simple. I've been very open about that since the beginning."

Cole's words ripped at my heart. We'd taken two steps forward, but my damn dad, Cole's stupid past, and his fears were pushing us three steps back.

"I don't know, Cole. I love you, but I don't know that I can keep hiding indefinitely." I reached for him but he stepped away.

"Then maybe it's better for all involved if we just cut our losses." Cole's beautiful eyes were dull and his face drawn.

"You want to break up?" My chest was going to explode, and I couldn't get a deep enough breath.

"I need something you can't give. You need something I can't give." Cole shrugged, but I knew he was fighting tears. "I've never loved someone the way I love you, but I won't give up the rest of my life for you."

"You don't have to! I'm not asking you to!" I roared. "Why won't you believe me when I tell you I know this town, I know these people? Several people already know and don't care. BJ will stand for you, we will back you."

Cole smiled sadly. "I wish I had as much faith as you do. But, my past says that if even a guy's own parents will turn on him, not much will stop virtual strangers from turning on him."

When Cole walked away from me, I stood for a whole five minutes in complete and utter shock. What the hell had just happened?

"Fuck!" The roar of my voice reverberated in Cody's office at the B & B.

"Whoa, man, calm down. Talk to us. What happened?" Cody laid a hand on my shoulder.

Levi stood at the door with a menacing frown and both hands on his hips as if waiting for the word to go beat someone's ass.

Jay watched me as if preparing for me to ransack the place.

When Cole walked away from me, I headed straight to BJ's to talk to Cody. My dad's sick laughter followed me from the shop. Levi was having lunch, and Jay showed up right as I got there. Cody had ushered us into his office for privacy.

My head pounded as if it was about to explode, my chest hurt, and I wanted to curl into a fetal position and cry until there were no more tears. But I was also angry. Angry as fuck.

Angry at my dad.

Angry at Cole.

Angry at myself.

"Where's Cole?" Jay asked warily.

"Who the fuck knows. After he told off my dad and broke up with me, I'm guessing he went back to school." I knew I was yelling and it wasn't helping anything, but I couldn't stop myself.

"Cole broke up with you?" Jay's eyes bugged. "And told off your dad?" He plopped down on the couch. "Whoa, start at the beginning."

Cody took his desk chair, I sat in a folding chair, which left Levi the floor or the couch. Positioning himself as far away from Jay as he could, Levi gave a disgruntled sigh and narrowed his eyes at Cody and me.

"Come cuddle, Daddy," Jay purred and launched himself toward Levi, wrapping his arm through Levi's and resting his head on Levi's shoulder.

If I hadn't been so distressed about Cole, I would have laughed my ass off at the look of sheer terror on Levi's face. The man finally gave up trying to get out of Jay's grasp, took a deep breath, rolled his eyes, and nodded at me to proceed.

"So, Dad was making all these drunken threats about ruining Cole's career or killing him. So, I stayed at Cole's last night to make sure Dad didn't act on it." I filled in details in case Jay hadn't heard yet. "Things were good between Cole and me this morning. Then, I guess he started really thinking about things at school and came up with some half-baked idea to talk to Ed. Cole showed up right after Kennedy's had been questioning Dad. Stalks right into Dad's office and polite as can be tells him to back off, leave him alone, and give the threats a rest. Tells Ed he won't be run out of town."

"Wow. That's pretty impressive," Cody interjected.

I couldn't help the smile that teased at my lips. "Yeah, I've never been so damn scared and so proud in one single moment in my entire life."

"I'm guessing Uncle Ed didn't take it so well?" Levi still looked appalled that Jay was hanging on his arm, but he seemed to have relaxed at least slightly.

"Understatement of the year. Pretty sure if Kennedy hadn't just been there, Dad would have reacted more violently." I ran a hand over my face as mental and emotional fatigue hit me like a freight train.

"So, how did Cole standing up to your dad lead to Cole breaking up with you?" Cody asked.

"Honestly, I have no clue. One minute we're talking and laughing about what he'd done in my dad's office, then the next minute he's saying we can't give each other what we need so maybe it's best to break up." I blew out a deep breath. "I mean, I thought him standing up to Ed was Cole's way of saying 'Fuck you all, I'm gay, I love Micah, and I'm going nowhere.' But that was clearly *not* what Cole was saying. In his mind, he told my dad to leave him and his job alone and that he wouldn't be run off. He feels that it's even more important to hide his sexuality now than before."

"You are both dumbasses." Levi shook his head in disgust and absentmindedly rubbed a hand on Jay's thigh before he realized what he was doing and jerked his hand back like he'd been burned.

"Yep," Cody agreed.

"Excuse me?" I wasn't really in the mood to spar with my cousin or my best friend.

"No. They're right. Cole is the bigger dumbass, but you both need a good smack to the head." Jay chimed in his two cents and snuggled deeper against Levi. "Don't worry, I'll take care of Cole. But you're going to have to do your part, too."

"What the hell did I do wrong?" I leaned my elbows on my knees and held my aching head in my hands.

"You agreed to hide and keep things secret. Then you moved waaay too fast in outing the relationship. Plus, you tried to rush Cole when he was dealing with a shit ton of emotional overload. He needed your support and promise that things were going to be okay and that you'd stand beside him." Jay clicked his tongue and his words hit me like a ton of bricks.

"And instead of being there the way he needed me, I expected him to turn right around and make our relationship public." Running my hands through my hair, I groaned. "Fuck."

"Now, don't take all the blame on yourself. Cole has a part in this, too." Jay gave Levi's arm a squeeze. "I'm going to head over and wait for Cole to get out of school. I'll be inviting myself to stay at his place tonight. Micah, you stay with Daddy-O here. I'll let you know when approaching Cole would be best." Jay stood, cracked his back, and stretched his long, lithe body like a ballet dancer. "In the meantime, think about what you're going to say. What you're going to do. Where you want this thing to go. What you're willing to sacrifice to get there."

And with that, Jay left the three of us sitting in stunned silence.

"How the fuck does some *kid* know so much and sound so smart all the time?" Levi growled.

"No clue, but he sure schooled our boy here. Hope he goes easy on Cole." Cody smirked.

"So, what am I supposed to say to Cole?"

"What are you willing to do? Give up?" Levi countered.

"Honestly, I'm willing to give up pretty much anything to be with him if it means not having to hide. I'll hide if that's the only way, because I love him so damn much. But I'd rather leave my job and BJ than give up on Cole." My words were firm and from the heart.

"Well, then, there's your answer. You know what *you* are willing to do and give up, but you're going to have to see if that meshes with what Cole is willing to do and give up." Cody shrugged. "Give him some space. Let Jay talk to him. And then see what you and Cole can work out."

"But, don't give up." Levi pointed a finger at me. "I've never seen you so happy and Cole does that for you. You two can work this out, even if it means you leaving BJ, but don't give up on someone you love."

I nodded. "I'm going to go crash at your place, Levi. I'm done at work for today." My head and heart couldn't take any more run-ins with my dad. And I needed a nap to ward off the all-over exhaustion that was threatening to destroy me.

"Okay. I'll be home late, but you're welcome to stay." Levi stood from the couch. "My last appointment should be done around ten-thirty tonight. I'll text Jay and tell him to make sure the security system is set at Cole's."

"Thanks, man." I pulled my cousin into a hug. "And sorry for interrupting your lunch rush, Cody." I hugged my best friend.

"Not a problem. That's why I have good people working for me. I trust them to run things when I'm not out there." Cody smiled and the three of us left his office.

CHAPTER 14

COLE

My eyes stung from unshed tears. My head was pounding. My heart ached.

And Jay was sitting on the hood of my car when I walked out after the last bell.

Fuck my life.

"Jay, I really don't have the energy for you today. I feel like shit. I just want to go home and sleep." I tossed a bag of schoolwork I knew I wouldn't touch into my backseat before climbing into the driver's seat in hopes that Jay would get the not-so-subtle hint and take a hike.

No such luck.

Of course.

"Sorry, Professor, I'm coming with you," Jay quipped as he folded himself gracefully into my passenger seat.

"The fuck you are. Today has sucked big donkey balls. I'm not in the mood." I didn't want to hurt the kid, but I needed to get home so I could curl in a ball and cry my eyes out.

"Too bad. I know what happened with Eddie Edwards. I know what went down with Micah. I'm not leaving. I'm here to save you from yourself and to help you and Micah fix the clusterfuck that you've found yourselves in." Jay reached for my knee and squeezed. "I know things suck right now. I know you want to be alone. I also know that's the last thing you need. So, drive on, good sir."

Jay's eyes were kind and his smile sympathetic, but the set of his jaw told me he wasn't planning on leaving. So, I put the car into gear and headed up Blueridge Hill.

"What are you doing?" I asked Jay as he punched buttons on the security system.

"Setting the alarm system. I'm staying here tonight. Levi wanted to be sure the alarm was set. You know, in case Eddie decides to make good on his promises." Jay finished arming the system and then sauntered toward the kitchen. "I'm starving. Whatcha got to eat?"

"Are you ever *not* hungry?" I grumbled.

Jay pretended to think about it, tapping his finger against his cheek. "No, I'm pretty much always looking for something to eat. Food, dick, ass...I'm always hungry for something." He waggled his brows and made a big show of licking his lips.

"How are you staying here tonight? Don't you have to work?" I scanned the fridge and found two bottles of hard cider. "You want one?"

"Nah, I'm going to drink that fabulous bottle of wine I saw on your counter. You can have the ciders." Jay opened a takeout container and sniffed. "How old is this?"

I peeked inside. Chinese. Rice, noodles, egg rolls, pork. "Um, how old does it smell?"

"It actually still smells damn good." Jay looked at me hopefully.

"I don't think it will kill you. Especially since it's not even smelling suspicious yet." I shrugged and grabbed two plates. "But you need to share."

"Fine," Jay huffed, but busied himself preparing the food. "And I'm skipping work tonight."

"You don't have to skip work for me."

"I know I don't *have* to. I want to. I got someone to cover for me. And, if I give him a good ass-eating, he may even split tonight's tips with me." Jay winked.

"You'd lick a guy's ass for money?" I gawked.

"Sweetie, I'd lick a guy's ass for free." Jay chuckled as he popped the leftovers in the microwave.

"You need to be careful. I'd hate to see you end up with the wrong guy and get hurt."

"I said I *would* lick an ass for free. Doesn't mean I actually do it. I talk a big game, but most of it is bogus bullshit." Jay grabbed the bottle of wine and set to work opening it.

Once we'd gathered our food and drink and settled on the couch, I was actually glad Jay was with me. It helped to keep my mind off of the day and losing Micah.

"Bitch, you screwed up big time. You're a fuckin' idiot." Jay's saucy reprimand was said with a smile around a forkful of Chinese food.

Well, having Jay around took my mind off Micah until he said that.

Fuck my life.

Groaning, I took the bait. "Okay, wise one, share with me your sage wisdom, teach me your ways, and direct me from my wrongs." I took a bite and then waved my fork at him. "How the hell is some teenybopper virgin so damn smart with relationship stuff? You're single for cryin' out loud."

"One," Jay held up a finger. "Sarcasm is not becoming on you. Two, I don't plan on being single long. Three, what I have to tell you may hurt or piss you off, but it's for your own good."

"Can I at least eat, shower, and get a couple drinks in me before you start?" I begged as I shoveled in rice and noodles.

"Of course. We'll finish the food, take showers, and enjoy our drinks. *Then* we will talk." Jay sipped his wine. "Oh, and sorry, showers will need to be separate. My heart belongs to another."

I laughed. "No worries." I paused at the ache in my heart. "Even if your heart was free to play, mine isn't."

"I know." Jay leaned in and kissed my cheek. "That's why I'm here. That and you have really good wine."

"Wait a second, are you twenty-one yet?" I removed the glass from his hand.

"No, but I will be in just a few short months." Jay pouted and held out his hand for the glass.

"Fuck, Jay, I really hate to say no. But, I'm an educator. I can't have an underage kid at my house and let him drink wine. Ever hear of contributing to the delinquency of a minor? I don't need one more thing the schoolboard can hold against me." I felt like a real shit not letting the kid drink, but *that* trouble was the last thing I needed.

"Fine. Whatever you say, Professor." Jay bounded from the couch. "Can I at least fix a milkshake?"

"Sure, I think there's ice cream and chocolate syrup." I finished my food and carried our plates to the sink while Jay mixed up milkshakes. Draining the first cider, I started in on the second bottle.

"Whoa, slow down there, buddy." Jay nodded toward the cider.

"Two won't do much. Plus, I want to have this one done so I can share in the milkshake." I waggled my brows. We were silent while Jay scooped and spooned and poured, but after the noise from the blender faded away, I spoke. "So, you have a thing for Levi, huh?"

Jay popped a hip. "Does the word *duh* mean anything to you?"

I smiled. "I mean, is it just the thrill of the chase? You just want what you can't have? You like him because he doesn't return the feelings?" I winced at the hurt look on Jay's face. "I mean, I don't *know* that he doesn't return the feelings. I haven't known Levi long, but you don't seem to be exactly his type. And I can't *ever* see Levi going for such an age gap."

"Sure the chase is great. The teasing is fun, but it feels like more than that. I've never been with anyone sexually. I mean, I've made out and done the whole hand jobs and blow jobs, but nothing more than that. But, never, ever has anyone made me feel like what I feel when I'm around Levi. He makes me feel safe. I feel like he sees me for more than just a pretty face and body." Jay's eyes filled with tears, but he quickly dashed them away with the back of his hand before pouring creamy, icy milkshakes into two beer mugs he'd pulled from the freezer. "Do you have any Kahlua? I could make yours a Mudslide."

I smiled at how quickly he changed the subject. "No, the ciders were enough for me." I took the mug and placed it back in the freezer. "I'll have mine after my shower." I headed from the kitchen before turning back to look at Jay. "Don't think this conversation is over."

"Done for now, but not over. I got it." Jay saluted me. "But, we have a more pressing situation to discuss tonight. Go take your shower and get comfy. I think we're in for a long night."

"Ugh. Jay, I have school tomorrow." I knew immediately that my protest fell on deaf ears.

"No, you're in need of a mental health day. You're calling in." Jay arched a brow obviously daring me to argue.

I started, but I knew Jay was right. I *did* need a mental health day. "Fine."

Jay smiled triumphantly. "Good boy, Professor. You get a gold star."

Rolling my eyes, I just shook my head and turned away. A long hot shower sounded amazing.

And I had a feeling I needed to prepare myself for whatever Jay wanted to talk about. I doubted he was going to sugarcoat any of it.

Fresh from the shower, I looked around the house for Jay but found him nowhere. For one panicked second I feared something bad had happened. Maybe Ed Edwards came and hurt him and was lying in wait for me.

Then I heard the singing. Loud, obscene, actually pretty good singing. I followed the sound to the basement where I found a just-showered Jay dancing around the open area with earbuds in while he sang a song I didn't recognize at the top of his lungs. I took a seat on the couch while his back was turned and settled in to enjoy the show.

The kid moved like liquid silver. All smooth and fluid. The grace of his body was mesmerizing. No wonder he was one of the hottest acts at Strip Teaze.

I could definitely see why men, and women, would pay money to watch him dance.

I was fully engrossed in the beauty of Jay's moves and his singing until he turned to find me watching him and screamed as if he'd been knifed.

Jay's hand went to his throat as he ripped out the earbuds. "Shit, Cole. You scared me to death." He blushed. "Sorry, I forgot I wasn't alone. I like to get a little lost in the music."

"No worries. You're good. That was amazing."

"Thanks." Jay climbed onto the couch and nestled himself comfortably as he faced me. "So, you screwed up with Micah."

I hoped we'd move on to small talk about his dancing to keep the focus off of me, but no dice. "So you've said." I rolled my eyes.

"What are you going to do about it?"

"What *can* I do about it?" I rubbed my brow in hopes of warding off the headache I knew was coming.

"Do you love Micah?"

"More than anything." That answer was easy, truthful, and came straight from my heart.

"Then you do whatever it takes." Jay shrugged as if it was the easiest choice in the world.

"I love him, but I can't lose my job." My heart hurt, and I felt pulled in two directions.

"First, I don't think you'd lose your job. This town, at least a large majority of it, thinks you're a great teacher and are happy you're here. Second, *I* can't tell you which is more important, a job or the love of your life. But you need to figure that out. If you work to keep your job you've basically told Micah to take a hike, and you may be outed one day anyway. If you work to hold on to Micah, you'll have his never ending love and support *if* you need it with the job issue."

I laid my head against the couch and closed my eyes. Letting Jay's words play over and over in my mind, I weighed the pros and cons against the risks and gains.

"Tell me what you're thinking?" Jay whispered.

"I'm thinking I really don't want to face life without Micah by my side."

"Then you need to talk to him, apologize, and get him back. Fight for what you had. And be prepared for whatever may happen with the school."

Jay's advice sounded so simple. "I don't know that it can really be that easy." I ran a hand over my face. "I blew up at Micah today and walked away from him and what we were building."

"Micah isn't completely innocent. He shouldn't have pushed and expected you'd be ready to move things ahead so quickly. I think he was just so happy to think about having you all to himself without having to hide." Jay smiled softly. "That man is head-over-heels in love with you."

I couldn't help the fluttery feeling in my heart and the goofy grin that graced my face. "Yeah? You think so?"

"I know so." Jay grabbed the remote. "Now, let's fold out this here couch into the bed it's been longing to be and start our movie marathon."

"We're having a movie marathon?" My jaw cracked with a gigantic yawn as I thought about trying to stay awake for that long.

"Well, *I'm* going to watch a movie. You're probably going to fall asleep within seconds of your head hitting the pillow. That's okay. Tomorrow, we can order from Cody's and lounge around the house all day." Jay helped me unfold the couch and make the bed with a spare set of sheets I found in a closet.

"Sounds like a fabulous plan." I crawled into bed. "When do I fix this thing with Micah?"

Jay seemed to think it over for a while, gaze locked on the TV. "We could put him out of his misery right now. He's at Levi's and probably hasn't stopped staring out the window at your house since he got there."

"But?" I sensed Jay didn't think that was the best idea.

"I think you both need a little time apart, a little time to think things through, and a good night's sleep." Jay clicked through the movie choices.

I agreed with Jay and started to tell him just that. But sleep took over much too quickly and I slipped into dreamland.

CHAPTER 15

MICAH

"Dude, did you sleep at all?" Levi wandered into the kitchen, stretching and wiping sleep from his eyes.

"Little." I answered without taking my eyes from the guest house.

"Did you sit there all night?" Levi chuckled and grabbed a cup of coffee as if he already knew the answer.

"Yeah." I didn't even bother denying it. I'd settled into my lookout spot as soon as I knew Cole and Jay were in the house, and I only let myself doze when I saw they'd turned off the lights. I figured if the alarm was set and they were sleeping, I could at least rest a little, as well.

"Everything seem to be okay?" Levi watched me with an obvious mixture of feeling bad for me and wanting to laugh at my stupid ass written all over his face.

"Yeah, I guess. I mean, no one went in or came out."

Levi sipped his coffee while leaning against the counter. "Maybe Cole and Jay found out they are perfectly compatible and hooked up."

I was out of my chair and chest-to-chest with Levi before he could even take another drink. "Shut your damn mouth. It's not like that."

"Whoa, calm down. It was a joke, man." Levi smirked. "I mean, don't get me wrong, I'd love if Jay found someone else to pester, but I'm not trying to ruin what you and Cole have. I was just giving you a rough time."

"Why does Jay bother you so much?" I stepped back from my cousin.

"Because he has nothing better to do with his life than mess with mine?" Levi rolled his eyes and shrugged.

"No, I don't mean why does he mess with you, I mean, why do you allow it to bother you?" I narrowed my eyes.

"He's a damn little pest. Always showing up and butting in. He's like a yappy little dog wanting to play with a big dog."

If he had stomped his feet in protest, Levi would have looked like an overgrown petulant child. "So, it has nothing to do with him getting under your skin and you finding yourself drawn to him?" I knew I was poking the bear, but I was sore and grumpy from sleeping in a kitchen chair all night while basically stalking the love of my life.

"Fuck no." Levi jabbed me with a finger. "Don't even say something like that."

I laughed. If I pushed too much I'd be going rounds with Levi's fists, but I couldn't stop myself. "Me thinks thou doth protest too much."

"Shut up. That *kid* isn't even close to my type. Even if he was closer to my age, I don't go for lithe, fragile, beautiful men. I want a guy I can rough up a little, someone I can hold tight and not be afraid of breaking. But, all of that aside, Jay isn't even twenty-one yet. We have *nothing* in common. He's got a crush, that's all." Levi's nostrils flared as he listed his arguments.

"So, you admit that he's beautiful?" I bit my lip to hide my smile.

Levi ran a hand over his face and groaned. "So god damn beautiful it hurts, but that's not the fucking point."

My heart caught in my chest at Levi's admission. I'd never seen my cousin so tormented by a guy.

"And I swear on all that's holy, I will deny it to my dying day if you ever tell anyone I just said that," Levi growled. "Jay and I would never work. We are too different in too many ways."

"Maybe you should stop fighting so hard and just see what happens. You may find that your differences work. Sometimes love has its own plan and you can't fight it." I spoke hesitantly, ready to duck if Levi lashed out with punches.

But, instead, he simply pinched the bridge of his nose. "No. As much as part of me wants to give in and stop fighting, a relationship wouldn't be right. He's just a kid."

"He's legally an adult. In just a couple months, he'll be twenty-one."

"I'm more than ten years older than him. It wouldn't be right." Levi's eyes held pain. "The whole town would think I'm some sort of cradle robber."

"Wait, so we can tell Cole not to worry about what the town thinks, but you're allowing the opinions of a few to rule your love life?" I frowned.

"Stop using the word love. I don't love him and he doesn't love me. If anything, it's a serious case of lust," Levi snapped, but then after a moment, he sighed. "And, maybe I'm using the town as a reason, because I'm running out of excuses."

"If it's just lust then stop fighting and let it happen." A thought raced through my mind. "Unless you're scared it's more than lust."

"Shut. The. Fuck. Up." Levi glowered. "It's lust pure and simple, but I don't want to get the kid's hopes up. I don't want to hurt him. Now, let's stop beating that horse and tackle your love life. Seems yours is the one in the most dire need right now."

My shoulders slumped and I sighed thinking about my riff with Cole. "You're right. I don't know how to fix it."

"You fight for it."

"What if there's nothing left to fight for?" Fear laced my words.

"Do you love Cole?"

"More than anything. I'd never thought of a future with one certain person, but Cole is all I can think about when I think of settling down."

"Then you don't let him go." Levi shrugged.

"*He* walked away. He's the one who ended things. Even if I don't want to let him go, how do I make him come back?" My heart and mind were a jumble of thoughts and emotions.

"If I know Jay he's been busy talking to Cole. I say we give them their day together and then you go over there and relieve Jay of his duty. Spend the evening with Cole, even if it's just holding him close and assuring him that you're willing to do whatever it takes." Levi looked at me pointedly. "But, you need to be *sure* you're truly willing to do whatever it takes. Can you deal with a secret relationship if that's what it comes down to?"

"I don't know, Levi. I swore I'd never hide. I want to be open and honest about who I am."

"Then, maybe you take today and think about your options. Be *you* and possibly lose Cole. Or keep what you and Cole have a secret and get to have him." Levi gave me a sad look.

"Both those options sort of suck." I rubbed at my chest as I thought about losing myself or losing Cole.

"Yeah, they do. But, if you love him, maybe one is better than the other."

"What about him loving me? Why doesn't he have to give up something to fight for what we have?" It was my turn to sound like a pouting child.

"Love doesn't keep score to make sure things are fair. Maybe this is your time to give up, to let go, to lose something. Cole may have to do the same. Maybe not today or tomorrow, but love is full of ups and downs, give and take. Cole's time may be coming." Levi clapped a hand on my shoulder. "Are you willing to fight even if you're the only one fighting for now?"

Levi squeezed my shoulder and left me standing in the kitchen with only my own thoughts for company. Picking up my phone, I scrolled through pictures of Cole and me. Those eyes, that smile. The taste of him on my lips. Laughing with him, loving him. Holding him in my arms and breathing in his scent. Were those things I could give up just because I wasn't willing to hide? Would Cole ever be willing to be out and open?

I could give up on Cole and lose him forever, and I'd always wonder what we could have become.

Or.

Or, I could fight for him, fight for us, fight for the special love we'd started building.

A verse my mother had hanging in the living room came to mind. *"Love is patient…"* I'd read that verse over and over and only found myself becoming angry with it. If my mother believed all of those things about love, why was she with an asshole such as my father?

But, I looked up the verse on my phone anyway and found 1 Corinthians 13:4-7.

Love is patient, love is kind. It does not envy, it does not boast, it is not proud. It does not dishonor others, it is not self-seeking, it is not easily angered, it keeps no record of wrongs. Love does not delight in evil but rejoices with the truth. It always protects, always trusts, always hopes, always perseveres.

Love is patient. Love keeps no record of wrongs. Love always hopes. Love always perseveres.

While I'd never really turned to religion or scripture during troubling times, I found relief and comfort in that passage.

I had my answer. I knew I'd fight.

But, would Cole be willing to do the same?

The sun was slowly slipping below the horizon when I stood at the guesthouse's door and knocked. Jay peeked through the curtain covering the small side window and smiled.

Opening the door, Jay crossed his arms and cocked a hip while batting heavily made-up lids and lashes. "Well, well, well. Who do we have here? What is the purpose of your visit kind sir?"

I just shook my head at Jay's theatrics. "I'd like to talk to Cole, please."

Jay pursed his lips and tapped a finger against his chin. "Just what are your intentions with my dear Cole?"

Beginning to get frustrated, I took a step forward. "Look, Jay, I'm not going to hurt him. I just want to talk to him. Apologize. See if we can fix this." The expressionless stare Jay gave me made my insides clench. "I mean, if Cole wants to fix it. Has he talked to you at all?"

"Ah, there's the desperation and determination I was waiting on. Fine, come on in. I'll gather my things and head out so you boys can have the evening together." Jay's hips swished as he sauntered down the front hall. "But, don't keep him up late. Cole has to work in the morning."

"What about me?" Cole's voice sounded from around the corner before he entered the hallway and stopped short. "Micah."

Jay moseyed up next to us while we stood and simply stared at each other. "Okay, you two boys play nice. I think I'll go show Levi my newest makeup trick before I head to work tonight." Jay winked before kissing us both on our cheeks. "Fight for it," Jay whispered in Cole's ear before walking away.

And then we were alone.

"Um, sorry. Where are my manners? You want a drink? Come sit down." Cole blabbered as he scurried into the kitchen.

"Yeah, I'll have whatever you're having." My eyes stung with tears. *Please let this work out. Please don't let it be the end.* I waited for Cole to hand me a bottle of water and then followed him to the living room.

When Cole took a seat on the couch, I took that as a sign it was okay to sit next to him. Lowering myself to the cushion only inches from him, I fought against the emotions trying to overtake me at his close proximity. I could feel his heat, and I could smell his familiar scent. I wanted to touch him, hold him, and taste him.

I took a long swig of water in hopes of gathering my thoughts and feelings.

"I'm sorry."

"I'm sorry."

Our words tumbled together like a mishmash of acrobats.

Pink cheeks, knowing smiles, soft eyes, we laughed at ourselves as we stared at each other.

"Can I go first?" I needed to get out my words before they exploded inside.

Cole simply nodded.

When I reached for his hand, I nearly choked on the electricity that raced between our bodies. Cole's slight squeeze was all I need to continue. "I'm sorry for the way things went down. I'm sorry for my dad's part in all of it. I'm sorry I automatically assumed you standing up to my dad meant you were ready to be out. I was wrong to do that." I took a deep breath, ready to beg Cole to allow us the chance to work things out.

"Wait, before you go on, I need to say something." Cole lifted my hand and kissed the back of it. "I'm sorry. I got scared. I overreacted. I walked away when I should have stayed and talked."

"What are you saying?" My heart nearly stopped beating while waiting for Cole's answer.

"I'm saying I'd like to fix this thing between us, fight for it...if you're willing." Cole held my hand between both of his.

A gush of breath I'd been holding rushed from my lungs. "Yes. Yes. Yes. A thousand times yes. I'm willing to work on this. I'm willing to fight for it." Crowding Cole back against the arm of the couch, I stopped myself mere millimeters from kissing him. "Cole Pierce, I love you. I will do whatever it takes to keep you in my life. Please don't ever walk away from us again."

Cole's eyes filled with tears. "Never. I'm sorry I can't be everything you need me to be right now."

Thumbing away the single tear rolling down Cole's cheek, I traced the moisture along his lips. "Shhh, right now you're everything I need. I'll never force you into something you're not comfortable with."

"But it's not okay for me to force you into keeping us a secret. That's not fair." Cole sniffed and lost the battle to keep his tears at bay.

The verse from earlier popped into my head. "Baby, love isn't about fairness. Love is about being patient. Love is about persevering. No timeline or deadline exists in our relationship." I moved even closer, my lips just a breath away from his. "We gotta do us. There's no right or wrong way to do that. We'll figure us out as we go along if you're up for it."

I only waited a split second for Cole to nod before capturing his lips with mine. With that one single connection, I was back home. For me, love was Cole in my arms. Love was our tongues dancing, dipping, and tasting. Love was the feeling of everything being right in the world as I wrapped my arms around him and whispered, "I'll never let you go."

"Let's go to bed," Cole mumbled against my mouth.

"You tired?" I didn't want to make the next day at school hard.

"Not yet." Cole winked and nibbled at my lip.

"Mmm, that sounds promising." I turned around and bent my knees slightly. "Climb aboard."

Cole laughed but jumped onto my back. "Where we going?"

"To turn off the lights, but I don't want to be away from you for even a couple minutes right now." I carried Cole around the house as he flipped the wall switches in the kitchen, living room, and hallway.

"You know, we'll have to be apart sometimes. At least for work." Cole teased his tongue along the shell of my ear.

"But, not for tonight." I headed toward the basement.

"Not for tonight," Cole agreed.

I stopped by the basement door. "Here's where your ride ends. I'd rather not end up at the emergency room because we tumbled down the stairs."

We toed off our shoes and stripped to just underwear in the dim light of the basement. Climbing onto the bed from opposite sides, we met in the middle as our bodies crashed together in a heavy mix of hot passion and lustful longing. And love. Always love. It was what made my time with Cole different than with any other man. Loved changed everything.

"God, baby, my hands can't touch you everywhere I want to touch you quickly enough." I groaned as my hands roamed over Cole's skin.

"Shhh, it's okay. We've got all night. We've got forever." Cole grabbed the back of my head and pulled me close for a long, slow, deep kiss.

When I moved my head to a different angle, something over Cole's shoulder caught my eye. "Hold that thought." I waggled my brow with a devious idea. Climbing from the bed, I pushed open the door to the bathroom and adjusted the basement light until the bed and Cole could be seen perfectly in the mirror's reflection. "Turn around." I slid off my underwear as I waited for Cole to turn his back to me and then climbed back onto the bed. Kneeling behind him, I nestled my dick against his ass before wrapping my arms around his chest and resting my chin on his shoulder. "Look at us."

Cole lifted his head and looked straight into the mirror, meeting my gaze. "Oh my god, we're beautiful."

"So fucking beautiful." I ran my hand down Cole's stomach and watched in the mirror as I palmed his rock solid cock. "Want these off. Want to see all of you wrapped in my arms." I hooked my thumbs in the front of his boxer briefs and pulled them slowly down his hips. Watching in the mirror, I held my breath as I waited for his cock to spring from its confines. "Damn, baby, look at you. So perfect, so hard for me."

Cole turned his head and reached his arms up to clasp both hands behind my neck. Pulling me close, he kissed me as I stroked his shaft and ran a thumb through his wet slit. Lifting my gaze to the mirror, I gasped into Cole's mouth as I saw his midsection tautly stretched and his throbbing cock fucking my fist.

"Fuck me, Micah." Cole rasped against my mouth. "I wanna watch you fuck me."

Turning our bodies slightly, I hurried to grab the lube and condoms from the bedside table. Rolling the latex down my straining dick was almost enough to have me shooting my load all over Cole's back, but I gritted my teeth and soldiered on. Slathering myself with lube first, I gently pushed Cole's back. "Ass up, baby."

Cole went to his elbows, curving his back inward so that his hips opened wide. Cole on display just for me was beyond gorgeous. I dribbled lube in his ass and ran my finger through it while I watched our bodies in the mirror. Cole's hungry eyes were on fire as he stared back at me.

"I need you in me. Now." He spread his legs wider and pressed himself against my finger.

"Good, because I need to be in you. Now." As I spoke, I pushed the head of my cock against his hole and gritted my teeth against the hot pleasure of Cole's body opening for me. With our bodies turned slightly, I could see our reflections in the mirror. My hands on Cole's hips, his ass rocking back against me, and my cock as it slid from his body before slamming back in. "I'm going to come so hard in you."

Cole raised up from his elbows slowly, keeping my cock deep in his ass, but pressing his back against my chest. Turning our heads together, we stared at our joined body. Running a hand down Cole's chest, I gripped his cock in my fist and pumped him with the rhythm of my dick fucking his ass.

"I'm going to come, baby," Cole panted.

Thrusting his cock into my hand and impaling his ass upon my dick, Cole whimpered and I felt his body tense. When his release coated my hand, I slammed deep into his ass and roared my own orgasm into his tight hole.

Cole fell face first to the mattress, taking me with him.

I caught myself on my hands for fear of squashing him.

Cole moaned, "No, lay on me. I want to feel you heavy on top of me."

Letting my full weight press against Cole's back, I kissed his neck and shoulder as I watched us in the mirror. "You are so fucking perfect." A kiss to his ear. "And gorgeous." A kiss to his neck. "And *mine*." A sloppy kiss landed at the corner of his mouth as he turned his face back toward mine.

Pulling from his body, I quickly disposed of the condom and rolled him into my arms. "I love you. No matter the fight, I'm in it to win it. I need you to know and understand that." I held Cole's face in my hands. "That means we do this thing together. No walking away if things get tough."

"I'm in it. I want to fight for it." Cole held my head in his trembling hands. "My pace may be a little slower than yours, but I love you too much to let go without a fight."

"Then we fight." After sealing our love and promise with a kiss, I slipped to sleep.

CHAPTER 16

COLE

I woke sore, stiff, and sticky. A small price to pay for having Micah back in my life. But not the greatest way to wake up on a school day. Groaning, I stretched against Micah and smiled when he pulled me close to his chest.

"Let's play hooky." Micah's words were rough with sleep and awfully tempting.

"Mmmm, that sounds like a fabulous idea, except Jay had me skip school yesterday." I snuggled into Micah's chest and purred like a cat when he ran his hands through my hair. "I won't have to worry about losing my job because I'm gay if I keep skipping school. I don't have that many sick or personal days to work with."

Micah pouted. "I don't like that Jay got a skip day and I don't."

"Awww, poor baby. You don't need to be skipping work either. You don't want to give your dad any more of a reason to withhold the shop from you." I kissed Micah's nose and rolled from bed.

"That fuckin' asshole won't ever give me the shop. I'll either have to buy it from Mitch or open up my own place," Micah grumbled into the pillow.

"What's Mitch doing? I've never seen him around the shop." I was truly curious about the mysterious older brother.

"Who the fuck knows. He shows up now and then, does some work at the shop, lets Dad think he's interested in inheriting the business, and then rides off into the sunset to who the hell knows where. Mitch is much more a city guy at heart. He has no reason to stay in BJ."

"Not even for the shop?"

"Nah, I think he likes stringing Dad along to fuck with us both. He's never been a fan of Dad, the town, the shop, or me. Mitch pretty much lives his life for only himself." Micah shrugged. "I mean, I guess it's not a bad way to live if you're able to do it without hurting anyone else in the process."

"So, you think Mitch would take the business just to piss you off?"

"Maybe. More than likely he'd take it and sell it to someone else. But I sure as hell plan on being in the buyers' pool if it comes down to it." Micah rolled from bed. "Let's shower and then coffee. I'll even make you breakfast." He winked and slapped my ass as we walked toward the bathroom.

"Aww, so sweet." I smiled as I turned on the shower.

Slick, soapy, sexy fun in the shower led to coffee and oatmeal at the kitchenette table.

As we stood side-by-side rinsing our cups and bowls at the sink, Micah reached for my hand. "Thank you for giving us a fighting chance. Thank you for giving me you."

I leaned over to kiss him, sweeping my tongue alongside his. "Thank you for fighting. Thank you for being patient. Thank you for standing by my side. I love you."

"Love you, too."

I left for work floating on air. I had the man I loved, a home, a job, a car. I felt like I could take on the world.

Good thing I was feeling strong. From the moment I walked into the school, my gut told me I was going to need every single bit of that strength.

FAGGOT

The slur scrawled on the whiteboard in my classroom was like a knife to my chest.

Glancing around the room and at the door to see if anyone was watching for my reaction, I quickly snapped a photo of the offense before erasing it and dropping into my desk chair with a defeated sigh. *And so it begins.*

Tears stung my eyes and fear gripped my stomach.

Before I could decide whether or not I should call Micah, Mr. Sutton appeared at my door.

"Pierce, I need to talk to you. See me in my office during your prep period."

Without waiting for me to answer, he walked away.

Two hours later, my head was pounding, I'd almost ground my teeth to the gums, and I almost wanted to carry a trashcan with me in case I upchucked my oatmeal from a breakfast that seemed eons ago. My first two classes were identical. There were three types of student reaction to the rumors that were obviously already making their way around school. The first kept their eyes down and didn't even acknowledge me. The second gave me sad looks of pity and sympathy. The third laughed, joked, and whispered gay jokes and slurs under their breath.

Heading to Mr. Sutton's office, I wondered if I'd even make it through the whole day.

"Pierce, come on in." Sutton called from his office when his administrative assistant let him know I had arrived. She and I both winced at the bark in his words.

"Close the door and sit down," Sutton demanded.

When I shut the door and sat in the chair across from my boss's desk, he templed his fingers in front of his face and stared at me for several moments.

Yeah, I am definitely going to puke.

"Mr. Pierce, I received a very disturbing phone call yesterday. Of course, I couldn't address this call with you then because you were out sick. And, while we're on that topic, let me remind you that we have a high attendance expectation for both students *and* staff here at Blueridge Junction High School."

He paused to let that bit of information sink in. Appropriately reprimanded, I swallowed and nodded before Sutton continued.

"The phone call I received wouldn't be a big deal in some cases. But, because of your constant contact with students in this town, I'm afraid it may become an issue."

I could tell Sutton wanted me to fill in the blanks and make his job easier. But I figured I could make him squirm just as much as he was making me. "Sir, I don't understand. What was the phone call about?"

"A concerned parent wanted to let me know about your, um, *different preferences*, um, in the area of, um, dating and relationships." Sutton sputtered through his feeble attempt to relay the concern.

"I'm not following, sir." It took everything in me not to smirk. I damn sure wasn't going to make it easy. Before Micah and Blueridge Junction, I likely would have blubbered a protest and promised anything asked of me to make sure everyone was comfortable and my job was safe. Something about having Micah and the guys on my side, having friends in the community, and standing up to Ed Edwards had lit a switch inside me. I wouldn't purposely put myself or my job at risk, but I definitely didn't plan on rolling over and letting hateful bigots walk all over me.

A flustered Sutton pinked even more as he dug at the collar of his dress shirt as if his tie was choking him. "The parent reported that there's a very good chance you're *gay*."

"Any chance this *concerned* phone call came from Ed Edwards?" I snarled. My insides flared with anger and panic.

"Who the phone call came from is not your business nor is it of any importance." Sutton puffed his chest. "What matters to me as principal of this school is that I keep the students safe. That's my responsibility to the community."

"And what does my rumored sexuality have to do with any of that?" Somewhere along the line, my backbone had strengthened. I pictured Micah sitting beside me as I spoke to Mr. Sutton.

"A rumor. Yes, yes, that's what I had hoped to hear you say." Sutton took a deep breath and sat back in his chair obviously relieved.

"And if it wasn't?" I nearly swallowed my tongue at my own bravery.

Sutton narrowed his eyes. "Wasn't what? Wasn't a rumor?" Leaning his elbows on the desk, he studied me. "Well, I'd have to encourage you to keep your private life just that. *Private.* Now, I don't have any problem with the gays, but I don't feel like it has any place in our schools. You're a good teacher and I'd like to keep you around. But, if it comes down to a school board decision, there won't be much I can do about it."

Taking a deep breath, I thought about my words before speaking. "So, I could be fired on the basis of sexuality?"

"No, no, I'm not saying that. This school district is an equal opportunity employer and we'd never get into the messy legalities of terminating an employee based solely on sexuality, gender, religion, disability or race." Sutton looked me straight in the eye. "But, the school board *can* terminate if an employee's evaluations and performance have been subpar or if it is determined that an employee is a threat to student safety."

My poor gums were going to be bleeding by the time I left the meeting. "My evaluations and performance have been stellar."

"Yes, well, let's hope they continue that way." Sutton nodded.

"Should I be worried about the school board deeming me a *threat* to student safety?" I summoned every bit of strength I had to keep my words calm and not sneer at the man.

Sutton sat back in his chair. "I feel like this discussion has met its purpose for today. I'd hate for you to be late to your next class."

Accepting that I had been dismissed, I stood. With a grim nod toward my boss, I headed toward the door.

"Pierce?" Sutton called out.

I turned and waited for him to speak.

"Just remember. Blueridge Junction is small. People watch and see things. Word gets around."

Fighting not to roll my eyes, I nodded at his threat veiled as advice and left the office.

"Pssst." An urgent whisper caught my attention.

Turning, I saw Mrs. Wilson, Sutton's secretary, sitting at her desk. She waved me closer.

"I just want you to know that not everyone in town or even in the school feels the way Mr. Sutton does," Mrs. Wilson whispered. "If it comes down to a fight, just know you've got quite a few people on your side." She winked and immediately went back to the paperwork in front of her.

I smiled briefly as I left her desk. But the giggles, whispers, and gawking as I walked back to my classroom mixed with the words Mr. Sutton had spoken and quickly brought back the feeling of dread.

Imagining Micah, Levi, Cody, Jay, and even Kennedy in my position, I took a deep breath and steeled myself for the rest of the day. I wouldn't roll over. I wouldn't hang my head. I mean, I wasn't going to shout my sexuality from the rooftops, but neither would I let Ed Edwards or anyone else badger me into leaving without a fight.

Two weeks later, my resolve was wavering.

School was on a break, and I was trying to relax and recoup, but the happenings of the last couple weeks had started to wear on me.

"So, still no idea who has done all the vandalism and threats?" Cody, hands on both hips in his living room, directed his question to Kennedy.

"No. We're pretty sure it's the same person or people involved with each incident, but we haven't traced anything to a suspect yet." Kennedy was clearly frustrated. "I mean, it's obvious the guy isn't a professional. He's sloppy. He's just not sloppy enough for us to nab him. Yet. But we will. We'll figure it out."

"How much more has to happen?" Micah snapped. "Cole's car was spray painted and all the tires slashed. A brick was thrown through his bedroom window. And a bag of burning shit was left at his front door. Each of these with a threatening note telling Cole to leave town." Micah gestured wildly with his arms. "These are hate crimes pure and simple."

"Believe me, I know. I'm as frustrated by all of it as you all are." Kennedy pinched the bridge of his nose.

"Are you keeping close tabs on Ed?" Levi had been sitting on the couch while Jay rubbed his shoulders, but all of a sudden Levi must have realized what he was letting happen and he jumped up to pace the room.

"Yeah, he's one we're watching closely. He's quiet, not doing or saying anything that could point to him." Kennedy shook his head. "But, I have no doubt he's somehow involved."

"I'd bet the shop on it," Micah growled.

I laid a hand on Micah's shoulder and he wrapped his arm around my waist and pulled me close.

"Listen," Jay piped up. "I need to head to work, but if there's anything I can do to help, please let me know."

"Since you know a lot of the students at the school, talk to them and get their feel for Cole teaching there." Kennedy's suggestion drew curious looks from all of us. "I just think it would help to know where the students stand. If they are supportive as a whole, that's a really strong support to have. And maybe one of them would be more likely to slip or give up a possible suspect rather than the police."

"Yeah, I can totally do that." Jay smiled broadly, brushing a floppy chunk of hair from his face before heading out the door.

Levi surprised the hell out of us by getting up to follow Jay out the door.

"Where you goin?" Cody smirked around his question.

"Just going to make sure he gets to work okay. I don't like all the hate crimes and threats around town lately. They are targeting Cole, but they may be open to the opportunity to hurt anyone. Jay isn't exactly threatening." Levi eyes narrowed more with each word as if daring us to say something.

We all knew Levi following Jay represented more than *just* the kid's safety.

"Good idea." Kennedy spoke up and broke the tension.

"I'm tired. I want to sleep until this is all over." I yawned.

"Come on, we'll go home." Micah steered me toward the door. "Kennedy, let us know if you find out anything. We need this fucker to screw up. Just once. Screw up and give us a clue to nail his ass."

I climbed into Micah's truck and snuggled close as he directed the vehicle toward Levi's house. In what had become a fairly normal routine, Micah pulled up to the guest house and jumped out to check the house while leaving me locked inside his running truck. Once he deemed it safe, Micah would motion me in and then go park in Levi's garage.

I'd given up on all of the hiding and secrecy. People already had the rumors and assumptions and their own opinions; I needed Micah and our friends too much to push them away just to keep up appearances.

"All clear. Come on, baby. You need to shower and get in bed." Micah held out his hand for me to climb down from the truck.

"Mmm, that sounds so good. I'll take a shower but only if you promise to meet me in bed." I leaned heavily against him and savored his warm strength as we walked toward the house.

"It's a deal. I'll meet you in bed after my shower. Don't try to stay awake on my account. I know you're exhausted." Micah kissed the top of my head. "Lock the door and arm the security." He watched while I locked the door and pressed the alarm keypad.

Even with all the shit going on, I couldn't help but grin like a goofball as I watched him walk toward his truck. Things sure had changed *for* me and *in* me since I met Micah and came to BJ. I shuffled my way down the stairs into the basement to shower. For some reason, the basement always seemed more protected, and ever since the brick thrown through the main floor's bedroom window, I had no desire to sleep anywhere with accessible windows.

Fighting to keep my eyes open as I went through the bare minimum motion of showering, I stumbled from the steamy bathroom to the bed Micah and I shared most nights. Before flopping myself down, I thought to check my phone. Glancing around the room in an exhaustion-induced fog, I struggled to recall where I had left the device.

Was it in the truck? Maybe Micah grabbed it.

Climbing the stairs, I headed straight for the main bathroom expecting to find Micah finishing up his own shower. But he wasn't there.

Entering the hallway, I called out, "Micah?"

No answer.

He should have been back from parking the truck by then.

A shiver traveled through me making the hairs on my neck stand up.

Glancing down the hall toward the main door, I saw it was still locked and the alarm still armed. But that made sense because Micah would have locked the door and reset the security system when he came in.

But, my shoes were the only ones by the door. If Micah had come in the front, he would have left his shoes on the rug like we always did.

"Micah?" Fear rattled through the word.

Maybe he just came in the back door. I spun around and crept toward the back of the house. The door was locked, the outside security light was dark—it would have come on if Micah came through that door—and again—no shoes on the rug.

Micah hadn't come back from parking the truck.

Levi wasn't home, so Micah had no reason to stay at Levi's after parking the truck. He should have driven into the garage, closed the garage door, and exited through the side door like he'd been doing for weeks.

I crouched and snuck back to the front of the house. Peeking out the front window, I saw that the garage door was closed but the side door was swung wide open.

Had Micah come out and forgot to close the door? Or had someone gone in?

With the thought of sleep pushed far from my mind, I swallowed the lump of fear in my throat and grabbed a fire extinguisher from the hall closet. As weapons went, it wasn't much, but I couldn't head into an unknown situation without some sort of protection

You shouldn't head into an unknown situation period, you idiot.

I could almost hear Micah's words, but I shrugged them off. No way was I staying in the house when something bad could have happened. I looked around one more time hoping to find my phone to call Kennedy or Cody, but I must have left it in the truck.

Slipping on a pair of tennis shoes with my flannel lounge pants and pulling a hoodie over my Blueridge Junction High School t-shirt, I crept out the door and down the stairs with my trusty fire extinguisher in hand.

Upon reaching the garage, I could hear nothing but the roar of blood in my ears as I snuck toward the side door. As I stepped into the dark garage, I groped blindly at the wall to my right for the light switch.

The next several moments played out in slow motion as if the entire scene was taking place in an aquarium of thick goo.

I flipped the switch.

The garage flooded with light.

I saw Micah.

On the ground.

In a pool of blood.

Too late, I heard the footsteps behind me.

And then my world went black.

CHAPTER 17

MICAH

"How is he?" Kennedy asked from the doorway.

I sighed. "Sleeping. They've got him dosed up pretty good with painkillers to help him rest." I stood from my permanent perch next to Cole's bed and spoke to Kennedy just inside the door. I wouldn't leave Cole's hospital room unless Cody or Levi were there, but I allowed myself to step away long enough to find out what Kennedy knew.

"Got anything?" I turned so I could watch Cole sleep while talking to Kennedy.

"We gathered up clues last night after Levi got home and called us. This morning a crew went back out to comb Levi's yard and garage for more evidence. Most promising lead we've got is the security system video. Levi obviously granted us access. We've got a tech crew running it to see if we can get any good images."

Kennedy was an imposing force and I was glad to have him on my side. "Any finger prints?" My question was for Kennedy, but I never took my eyes from Cole. The dull ache in my head was nothing compared to the heartache in my chest as we waited for Cole to heal.

I'd gone a little ballistic when we ended up in different ambulances. It took Cody and Hank holding me to the bed before I gave in and let the ER doctor check me out. I knew Levi and Jay were with Cole in some exam room, and I trusted them to keep him safe, but it didn't make me any less determined to get to him. Once the ER doctor cleared me with instructions for how to care for a concussion, I had bolted to Cole's room and hadn't left for more than a restroom break since the night before.

"A couple partial prints, but nothing solid. And nothing is matching up with the database. So, pulling a good image from the video is our best bet right now. If we can show it around town, maybe we can scare the perp out or get someone to talk." Kennedy turned to glance at Cole. "Doctors think he's going to be okay?"

"Overall, yeah." I walked back to the bedside and took Cole's hand in mine. The warmth of his skin was reassuring. "He's going to be sore for a while. Broken ribs, broken nose, fractured collarbone, and a major bump on the head from whatever the guy hit him with."

Kennedy winced. "Think it was a crowbar."

"Fuck." My gut churned with the memory of waking up in a pool of my own blood, the pounding explosion in my head, and the sight of Cole's seemingly lifeless body on the cold garage floor.

A nurse popped in to check Cole's vitals and record the pertinent information. "Mr. Edwards, I need to remind you that if Mr. Pierce's next-of-kin shows up, I will have to have you leave." She scolded me but winked at the end of her speech.

I nodded before she left.

"Exactly how did you get in here?" Kennedy narrowed his eyes. "You're not married, and you're not family."

"Well, nothing short of a bulldozer could have pushed me out, but Levi and Cody explained that Cole has no family here. Perk of a small town hospital, I guess. I went to high school with a couple of the nurses. They let me stay under the pretense that they'd called Cole's family and I'd have to leave if they showed up." I smirked.

"Did they call Cole's family?"

"Nah. Cole didn't have any contact info on him. And I sure as hell wasn't going to give them a number even if I knew one." I squeezed Cole's hand. "I'm his family. The BJ Boys are his family. We're all he's got and all he needs."

"He's got more than just you and the boys. He's got most of this town supporting him." Kennedy pulled over a chair from the corner to sit close to me. "Can you tell me again what you remember from last night?"

My head ached, I was exhausted, and I just wanted Cole healed and home, but I drew a deep breath. "I'm not sure it's anything more than what I told you last night. I left Cole at the house and drove the truck to Levi's garage. Pulled in, shut the door behind me, and checked my email and texts on my phone for longer than I meant to. The overhead light went out so I was stumbling around in the dark to get to the side door. I heard something behind me, turned to see what it was, and the next thing I know my head is exploding and I'm out cold."

"You didn't see who it was?" Kennedy had his notepad out taking notes.

"No. I had a brief glimpse of black in the little bit of light coming in through the windows, but that's it. I don't remember anything until Levi came home. He called 911 and got me to come to even though I was severely groggy and in major pain. I didn't realize Cole was in the garage until Levi moved from me to him." I stopped to clear the emotion clogging my throat. "I forgot every bit of pain I felt when I saw him on the ground. I thought he was dead. Why the hell had I taken so long to check my phone? Why the hell had Cole been stupid enough to come looking for me? Who the hell would want to hurt us so badly just because we're gay?"

"Listen, I'm going to let you rest. I'll need to talk to Cole when he's up for it. See if he remembers anything about the attack."

Kennedy stood, and he clapped a hand on my shoulder.

Standing, I pulled him into a hug and whispered gruffly, "Thank you for keeping me updated. Please find whoever did this."

"We will." Kennedy returned the hug before gazing down at Cole. "I think he's going to have another fight to face when he gets out of here. But, I think this one will be more evenly matched."

"What do you mean?" I frowned.

"Either Cole gives up and leaves like the perp wants him to, or Cole takes a stand and fights for his job and you." Kennedy shrugged. "I'm not sure which he'll do or which is the right thing, but if he stands to fight, he has almost the whole town on his side. The department has talked to ninety percent of the residents and they all want to see the violence end and Cole continue teaching at the high school."

"That's really good to hear." I smiled for the first time since waking up to the nightmare. "But, after this, Cole may decide he needs to start over."

"And? What will that mean for you?"

"I'll go anywhere he wants to go." I squeezed Cole's hand again and knew in my heart I'd leave town in a split second if that ended up being what Cole needed.

"That's what I thought." Kennedy laughed and reached out to clasp my and Cole's hand in his. "He's lucky to have you. I'll keep you posted."

And then I was alone with Cole. Alone with my pain. Alone with my fear. Alone with the extreme exhaustion. I held Cole's hand to my lips and placed soft kisses all over his bruised skin. "Cole, baby, I'm glad you're resting, but I need to see those beautiful eyes. I need to hear your voice and see you smile. God, Cole, I need you so much. Heal that gorgeous body of yours and then wake up for me. We'll get everything figured out. Where you live, where you work, we'll figure it all out and I'll be by your side for all of it."

The squeeze to my hand was almost imperceptible, but I took it as a sign that Cole was in there somewhere and would wake when ready. Laying the good side of my head on the hospital bed, I allowed myself to doze as I kept Cole's hand in mine. I knew the nurses wouldn't let me sleep too long due to the concussion, but I needed a few minutes of shut eye.

"Dude, go take a walk." Levi stood behind me and rubbed my shoulders. "They just dosed him again. Cole's going to be zonked for at least a couple hours. Better yet, go home and shower. Eat some real food. Order him something crazy for when he wakes up, but just get out of this room for a while before you go insane."

"I'm already insane, and I'll stay that way until he's awake and healed," I grumbled, but the thought of a shower and food sounded like absolute bliss. I still had grease from the garage floor and blood stains on my clothes.

"They are purposely keeping him out while his injuries heal. If he was awake right now, he'd be in tons of pain." Jay laid his hand on my shoulder. Whether to comfort me or touch Levi, I wasn't sure.

"Promise you'll be here the whole time and call me the second there's any update?" I hesitated.

"Yes, of course. Now go." Levi pushed me out of the chair. "Be careful. Wait, are you okay to drive?"

"Yeah, I'm fine." I shrugged him off. Now that my mind was made up to get a shower and food, nothing was going to stop me unless Cole woke up.

By the time I reached the parking lot, I realized I didn't have my truck.

"Need a ride?" Cody hollered from his car as he pulled up beside me.

"This is either a huge coincidence or Levi called you." I chuckled but barely had the energy to do even that as I climbed into Cody's car.

"Levi called, but I was already on my way over." Cody slapped my knee. "Let's get you some food and a shower."

I slept briefly in the car while Cody ran into BJ's to bag up food.

Once I'd showered and eaten, I was starting to feel human. But I was also starting to feel guilty for being out of the hospital while Cole was still there.

"Hey, wherever your mind just went, bring it back." Cody glanced at me over his shoulder as he scooped coffee into my coffee maker. "Cole is going to recover. He's getting constant monitoring. And the sleep is allowing his body to heal without feeling the pain. He wouldn't expect you there twenty-four seven." Cody grabbed two mugs from the cabinet. "We'll have some coffee and then you can go back."

I took a deep breath and let Cody's words calm me. "Sounds good." Seeing my laptop on the kitchen table, I remembered what Levi had said about ordering Cole some crazy gift for when he woke up. A cup of coffee and thirty minutes later, I had placed my order. *Thank goodness for same-day delivery.*

Cody poured me another cup. "One more, then we'll hit the road."

I nodded, too tired to argue much. But the caffeine was beginning to help. "Have you heard from Kennedy?"

Cody's head snapped up. "No. Why? Why would I hear from Kennedy?"

Scowling at him, I explained, "Oh, you know, since he's a police officer investigating the case of my boyfriend getting attacked, and he's your friend, I thought maybe you two had talked."

"Kennedy Marks isn't my *friend*," Cody growled. "We barely tolerate each other. He's hardheaded and bossy-as-fuck. No way we'd ever be friends. Acquaintances is about as close as we'll ever be."

I watched Cody for a moment while I sipped my coffee. The realization came to me slowly but once it got in my head, I couldn't help but laugh. "Oh my god, *you* like Kennedy."

"Fuck off. That's totally not true and not even the point." Cody jumped from his chair and all but threw his mug in the sink. "You ready to go?"

Smiling at my best friend, I just batted my lashes in my best Jay impersonation. "Mmmm, no. I think I'll savor this coffee a little longer. It's really helping to bring me back to myself. Thanks for making sure I got a shower and food."

Cody rolled his eyes and huffed as he plopped back into his seat. "Yeah. Sure. No problem."

"So, while I enjoy this delicious coffee, let's chat." I smiled deviously and waggled my brows. "How long have you liked Kennedy?"

Cody slammed a fist on the table. "Damnit, Micah. I don't like Kennedy."

"Hmmm, I bet two alpha men like you and Kennedy would butt heads and go round and round." Biting my lip, I pretended to ponder the relationship. "I mean, you'd probably eventually figure it out, but you're bound to fight in the process." I put my cup down and rubbed my hands together dramatically. "This is something I've *got* to see. Two leather daddies like you and Kennedy will be sexy entertainment at its best."

"Shut it. You make it sound like we're going to put on a stage show and charge admission. It's not like that," Cody grumbled.

"Ahh, but you do admit there is an *it* between the two of you." I clapped my hands together in glee. "This just keeps getting better and better." Standing, I poured the rest of my coffee down the drain. "Now, can you get me back to the hospital?"

"'Bout time. I'm sure Cole would love to know you've been away from his bedside so long just so you could give me shit about something that *doesn't even exist.*" Cody grabbed his keys and headed out the door.

"Oh, Cole won't be upset at all. But, he's going to be *very* interested in the information I've been able to gather." I paused when Cody turned around to give me a death glare, but I'd grown up with him so it didn't faze me much. "In fact, as serious as this whole situation is with the hate crimes and attack, I think you and Kennedy are the perfect little bit of levity to share with Cole and hopefully help him smile. I mean, smiling has to be helpful in healing, right?"

"Oh god, just shut up. There is *no Kennedy and me.*" Cody growled and stomped toward his truck.

"Mmhmm, you keep telling yourself that." I sing-songed behind him. "Just like Levi swore there was no him and Jay."

Cody's face blanched as he turned to face me. "No way. Levi and Jay are *nothing* like Kennedy and me." A split second after he spoke, Cody realized his mistake. "I mean, if there *was* a Kennedy and me, we'd be completely different than Levi and Jay."

"Uh-huh." I winked. "There are definite differences, but both relationships are ones I'd pay good money to see play out."

Cody set his jaw and opened his truck door before pointing his keys at me. "You need to worry about you and Cole and stop being so concerned about others' love lives."

"Oh, so now it's your love life?" I threw my head back and laughed at the panicked look on Cody's face. "Perfect!"

"Just stop talking. Stay out of it. Kennedy and I would be a bad idea. End of story." Cody peeled out as he headed the truck back toward the hospital.

CHAPTER 18

COLE

"I want a tattoo." Jay's saucy voice infiltrated my sleep.

"I want a million dollars, doesn't mean I'm going to get it." Levi snapped back.

Mentally scanning my body, I knew I was in pain, but it wasn't agonizing. The grogginess in my head made me think I was likely pretty doped up. Afraid to move, I laid still and drifted in and out of sleep while listening to Jay and Levi spar for the next several moments.

"You're the best artist in town. I want your work on me."

Jay was pouting. I didn't even have to see his face to know that voice.

"I'm the *only* tattoo artist in town. I don't work on minors." Levi bumped into my bed as he shifted his position. Cracking my eye slightly, I took stock of the room. My initial thoughts had been correct. Hospital, but why? Clearly I was hurt, but my brain was too foggy to remember what happened.

"I'm so totally *not* a minor."

"You're not twenty-one. In my book, that makes you a minor."

Levi was likely giving Jay a brooding scowl.

"So, you'll ink me when I'm twenty-one?"

Jay was huffy.

"I'll consider it."

"Thank you!"

The air in the room moved, and I knew Jay was probably dancing.

"I said I'd *consider* it," Levi growled.

"You'll consider what?" A voice asked from afar. *Micah*. Just hearing him made me feel calmer, less worried, and safe.

"Levi said he'd give me a tattoo once I'm twenty-one." Jay happily filled Micah in.

"Oh my god, I did not. I said I wouldn't even consider giving you a tattoo until you were at least twenty-one." Levi pushed up from what I was guessing was a chair. Funny how well I'd gotten to know these men that I could picture their movements and expressions even with my eyes closed. "I'm leaving, Jay. If you need a ride, you better come with. If not, you're on your own."

"Okay, Daddy. Just let me grab my stuff." Jay laughed.

Levi grumbled and left the room.

"You look better, Papi." I heard Jay land a smacking kiss on Micah's cheek. "Take care of the Professor, okay? I have to go before my grumpy-gus Daddy leaves me."

"Something tells me he'll wait." Micah laughed.

"Oh, he'll wait all right. He doesn't want to, but he can't fight it. I'll make sure it's worth the wait." Jay whispered as if telling a government secret. "Ohhhh, what's in the box? Did you bring presents?"

"I brought a present for *Cole*." Micah chuckled. "Go on. Go catch up with Levi."

When the room was quiet, I listened carefully to figure out where Micah was standing. "Hey, baby. I brought you a gift and some gossip. I thought I'd use them to wake you up, but you've been awake since I got here. Open those beautiful eyes for me."

Turning my head slowly, gauging the pain level, I opened my eyes. The glare of the room was blinding, but I could see my man, my Micah, plain as day standing beside my bed.

"Hey, babe. God, I'm glad you're awake. I've missed you so much." Micah leaned down and I pulled away as quickly as possible.

"Who are you? Why are you in my room?" It took every single bit of energy I had in me at that moment to pull it off.

Micah's eyes bugged. "Oh my god, you don't remember me?" He sat heavily the chair, dropping the box and running a hand through his short hair.

"That's okay. We can work on it. The doctor's said you may have some short term memory loss."

Gritting my teeth to keep from laughing, I continued with my charade. I didn't plan to let it go on for long. "Maybe I'd remember who you are a little quicker if you gave me my present."

Micah's eyes were on me in a second. "Oh, you think a present would jog your memory, huh?" I saw the sparkle in his gorgeous eyes and knew he was on to me.

"Yep. A present and juicy gossip may be just what I need to restore my memory." I finally cracked a smile and couldn't help the laugh that escaped. "Oww, it hurts to laugh." I grabbed what I assumed were broken ribs. "Shit. That totally backfired."

"You're an ass, Cole Pierce. I was running all kinds of terrible scenarios through my head. Like, what if you never remembered me and fell for Jay? Or you forgot all of your past and decided you wanted to go back to your parents' town?" Micah shook his head. "That was downright cruel."

"I'm sorry." I pretended to pout. "You can give me my present to make things better."

"How would *me* giving *you* a present make up for the shit trick you just pulled?" Micah teased as he waved the box around.

"It would make me feel better and I wouldn't have time to be mean to you?" I tried my luck.

"Look who's awake," Kennedy announced from the door.

Micah held the box in front of me like he was teasing a little kid. "Present and gossip later. Official police business first."

"You feel up to answering some questions?" Kennedy dragged a chair over and pulled out his notepad. "What do you remember from last night?"

I nodded and glanced at Micah then smiled.

"Don't even. It was bad enough you did it to me. I don't think Officer Marks would appreciate your little act." Micah poked a finger at me.

"Fine." I kissed the air toward Micah and turned to look at Kennedy. "I was exhausted. Just wanted to shower and go to bed. After my shower, I realized Micah wasn't back from parking the truck and that seemed strange. I grabbed a fire extinguisher and headed toward the garage because something wasn't right."

"Damnit, Cole. What the hell were you going to do with a fire extinguisher? You should have just stayed put and you wouldn't have gotten hurt." Micah rubbed a hand over his face.

"Water under the bridge now. I wasn't going to just go to bed wondering where you were. I wouldn't have been able to sleep anyway. And something just seemed wrong." I reached for Micah's hand and continued my story. "When I walked through the side door, it was dark in the garage, so I felt around for the switch. Once the light was on, I saw Micah on the floor and then someone knocked the shit out of my head." I reached to rub the gigantic bump on my skull.

"Did you see the guy?" Kennedy probed.

"No, he was behind me. I came to a couple times while he was kicking me, but I was more concerned with tuck and cover than checking out his mug. Sorry." I tried to shrug, but my shoulder area was throbbing. "Fuck, you think the nurses can get me any more pain medication?"

"Yeah, they've got you hooked up to a self-administering pump for right now. You can press that button now that you're awake and dose yourself up." Micah gestured to the device to my right.

"Nice." I pressed the button and prayed like hell the meds would kick in soon.

"Do you remember anything else?" Kennedy seemed to be wrapping up his visit which was good of him since I wasn't feeling the greatest.

"I don't remember when he said it, but the guy told me something to the effect of 'Better get out of town or the next time you won't live to make it to the hospital.' Or something sweet like that." I tried to laugh it off, but the threat still spooked me.

"Okay, I'll let you guys get some rest." Kennedy stood. "Lover boy here has a concussion so don't let him do too much." He pointed to Micah. "Take it easy. Call me if you remember anything else. I'll keep you both updated on what we learn."

"Awww, my poor baby. Here I was teasing you when you've got a concussion. I guess I thought since you were in street clothes and in my room you were fine." I winced as I recalled the blood on the garage floor. "But of course you're not fine. You were on the ground, passed out, and bleeding."

"No worries. I've got a headache, but that comes with the concussion." Micah shrugged.

"There was so much blood." I scooted over, wincing against the pain, to make room on the bed for Micah to sit.

"Head wounds tend to bleed a lot. I'm fine." Micah sat down next to me. "Now, which do you want first? The present or the gossip?"

"Ohhh, why you gotta make me decide." I rubbed my hands together. "Ummm, let's do gossip first."

Micah smiled and leaned closer. "Okay. You're not going to believe what I heard."

I loved how excited he was. "What?"

"I heard…," Micah glanced around as if he was trying to keep the secret just between the two of us in the otherwise empty room. "…that Cole Pierce is gay. Can you believe it?"

I smacked him on the shoulder. "That's not fair. You made me think you had real gossip."

"You made me think you forgot who I was," Micah taunted.

"Fine. We're even." I pouted. "Do you even have any gossip?"

"Yes. Cody and Kennedy." Micah nodded smugly.

"And?" I was waiting on the punchline.

"They sort of have a thing. I mean, they aren't admitting it, but they are totally into each other. Can you imagine the round and round those two will give each other?" Micah waggled his brows.

"This is not news, babe." I scrunched my nose.

"What? You knew Cody and Kennedy had a thing?" Micah looked surprised.

"Well, I mean, the tension and attraction rolls off of them in waves when they are around each other, so yeah, I guess I sort of knew." Micah and I continued to dance around the elephant in the room being that his dad could have been the attacker. My heart and head weren't into a serious discussion so I allowed the conversation to steer clear of the scary parts of the situation.

"But they hate each other." Micah scoffed.

"Love and hate are sometimes hard to distinguish." My lids were getting heavy and my tongue felt as if it was a size too big.

"I mean, I gave them a rough time about their hatred for each other and teased them, but I really never saw it until I talked to Cody earlier." Micah remained in stunned amazement.

Sleep was taking over. "Mmmm, can you imagine the two of them all decked out in their leather fighting for who's going to be sub for the night?" I yawned. "That would be so damn hot."

Micah laughed and squeezed my hand. "Hey, you want your present before you sleep?"

"Later…," was all I could mumble before I was out.

I awoke to voices.

"I'll do whatever he needs me to do." Micah's words were on edge. "I can't lose him."

"What about us and BJ?" Levi asked.

When I struggled to sit up in bed, I released a pained groan and the conversation stopped.

"Hey, how you feeling?" Micah rushed to my side.

"Better actually. Still sore, but I feel less groggy and out of it." I worked my arms and legs to remove some kinks. "I'm ready to get out of this bed."

"Let's wait until the doctor gives the okay for that." Micah grabbed the box from the side of the bed. "You want your present now?"

"I'm going to go," Levi interrupted. "Good to see you awake." With a brief nod, he was gone.

Micah laid the box on my lap. "I cut the packing tape to make it easier to open."

"When did you order this?" I pulled a rectangular gift box from under the packing bubbles.

"This morning when I went home to shower and eat." Micah grinned.

"And it's here already? Wow. Impressive." I slid a thumb under the box lid. Lifting the lid, I found six neatly arranged pairs of socks. "Awww, you got me socks."

"I got you socks."

"That's so sweet. I *love* new socks." I picked one pair up and rubbed the soft texture against my cheek.

"I remembered you saying you loved new socks, but look more closely at them." Micah nodded toward the box.

Each pair of socks was designed with a city name and landmark or a sporting team.

San Francisco.

New York.

Chicago.

Paris.

London.

Miami.

"Why did you get me six pairs of city socks?" I was genuinely confused.

Micah sat close, facing me and took my hand. "Each of those represents a city you could choose to move to. A fresh start if you need it. And, if you'll have me, I'd go to any of those cities with you. I'd travel to the ends of the earth if it meant being with you."

I ran my hand over the socks and processed Micah's words. "So, you think I should leave town?"

Micah shook his head. "What I think you should do is whatever feels right to you. Stay or leave, I'm by your side. But, if you go, I want you to know I have no problem going, too."

Tears flooded my eyes. "I love you so much. Thank you."

"You're welcome." Micah kissed my cheek. "So, where will it be? San Francisco? Miami?"

I paused to think about his question. My decision came easily. "No."

"Okay. What about Paris? I can learn French." Micah teased.

"No, I mean *no* I'm not leaving." My voice was strong and determined.

"It's okay if you want to."

"I'm not running. I want to fight it, fight them. I won't leave because of their threats. And if my job comes into question, I'll fight it, too." My decision gave me a giddy shot of energy through my pain. "I'm done. BJ is my home and it's where I want to stay."

"Then we stay and fight." Micah wrapped me in his arms and hugged me softly. Light kisses feathered my face. "I love you."

"I just wish we knew who was behind everything." Micah grumbled from the couch as the six of us ate pizza in Levi's living room.

"At least everything stopped." Jay shrugged as he picked a mushroom from his pizza.

"Yeah, it's stopped for now. But we only have suspicions on who was behind it. And it could start up again any second." Micah reached for my hand.

Two weeks had passed since I got out of the hospital. I was mostly healed, just a little sore still in the ribs and a few stiff muscles to work out in the mornings. The swelling in my nose had finally gone down, and I was beyond happy to get the nasal packing removed.

Not a single bit of graffiti, vandalism, or physical violence had taken place since the night of the attack. We all had our suspicions that Ed Edwards and the new tenant above the shop, Meth Boy, were in cahoots and had something to do with all of it. But there were no clues, no evidence, no witness statements pointing to Ed and Meth Boy. We only had our guts to go on.

"The fact that Meth Boy moved out, supposedly left no forwarding address with Ed, and the former landlord gave us a name that shows up as a person who died four years ago gives me a real funny feeling the two of them are involved." Levi took a huge bite of pizza before picking up the mushrooms Jay had discarded.

"Yeah. And Eddie has gotten awfully quiet lately. I mean, I know he's chatting it up around town with folks, but he's not said more than two words to any of us for two weeks." Cody shook his head. "Seems to me like he's toeing the line."

"He was very defensive the first time I questioned him. By the next time we talked, he'd mellowed and actually told me how *worried* he was about all the crime in BJ lately." Kennedy rolled his eyes.

"Well, I'm just glad things seem to have calmed down. Most the chatter at the school is gone. No more slashed tires or broken windows or slurs on my whiteboard." I wiped my greasy fingers on a napkin and went back to cuddling with Micah. "And thank goodness no more fiery bags of shit."

Cody's phone began to vibrate, Kennedy's phone beeped, and my phone's ringtone played.

Glancing around the room at each other, the three of us answered and retreated to different rooms to escape the audience and the noise.

"Hello?" I recognized the number as Mr. Sutton's.

"Mr. Pierce. I wanted to give you a courtesy call to let you know you'll be on paid leave from your teaching position until a school board meeting can be held in one week. Upon the decision of the board, you will either be dismissed, allowed to resign, or reinstated."

Heart heavy, I sank to the bed in the spare room. "I'm sorry, can you repeat all of that? It sounded like you just told me I'm not allowed to teach until the school board has a hearing about me?"

"Too many complaints have been coming up. The board just wants to be sure you're given a fair chance to state your side, and the town is given a chance to let their opinions be heard."

Un-fucking-believable. I pinched the bridge of my nose. "And what should I be doing in the week leading up to the school board meeting?" Would I need a lawyer? Did I even want to go through with any of it? Maybe I should just take Micah up on his offer to leave town and never look back.

"I guess if you're wanting to keep the job, you should gather evidence of your performance. Probably wouldn't hurt to get some students and community members to speak on your behalf."

Sutton cleared his throat. "I may not be keen on you being gay, but I think you're a good teacher. It's not my place to take sides, so don't expect me to speak one way or the other. If I'm called on in the meeting, I will be reporting facts only. But I'd like to see you stay at Blueridge Junction High School."

"Even though I'm gay?" It was the first time I'd spoken the words to anyone in BJ besides the guys.

Sutton coughed and sputtered. "My view of you is as an educator. I'd prefer not to discuss any of your personal life. And, as your superior, if the board deems you fit to stay on at my school, I'd ask that none of your personal life disrupt the learning of our students."

Shaking my head and rolling my eyes at Sutton's very clear meaning in his non-answer, I curled my lip and took a deep breath. "Okay. Well, then. Good luck finding a substitute. I'll see you at the board meeting in a week."

Hanging up, I stared at my phone for several seconds before I heard Micah explode in the living room.

"This is complete and utter bullshit!"

I returned to the room to see Kennedy and Cody had also ended their calls.

"Let me guess. You heard about the school board meeting?" I smirked. It was either joke and smile or I'd break down crying.

"Yeah, Dad called to tell me. Heard it at the B & B." Cody grimaced.

"My captain called to let me know. Said we'd likely have a show of officers at the meeting, but he said I can choose to be off-duty that night if I'd like to support a friend." Kennedy winked and slapped a hand on my shoulder.

I returned to my seat and so did everyone else.

Jay curled his legs up under him as he perched on the loveseat. "So, what are you going to do?"

Five pairs of eyes turned to me.

Micah reached for my hand.

I took in the room full of men I called friends, men I knew had my back, took a deep breath and shrugged. "A few years ago, I would have packed my bags and moved out of town. And, who knows, maybe I'll still do that in the end. But this time I won't leave without a fight. I won't give up without standing up for myself and for those like me who think they have no option but to hide."

"Then we fight." Micah nodded and his smile warmed my heart.

"And we'll be standing with you."

Levi's words were solid and genuine. I knew I had five upstanding, respected, and strong men standing with me.

"Hell to the yeah we will." Jay cheered. "I think we should all get tattoos for the meeting. Like matching ones to show our solidarity."

"That's ridiculous." Levi bopped Jay on the back of the head.

"Okay, six matching tattoos would be dumb. How about you just tattoo me before the meeting?"

Jay smiled and raised his brow in hopeful anticipation.

"Good Lord, do you ever give up?" Levi asked.

Cody snorted.

"Nope." Jay popped the *p*. "Admit it Daddy, your resolve is starting to weaken. You're wearing down. Soon, you'll be putty in my hands."

"The fuck I will," Levi growled. "I've told you, it ain't gonna happen. You may be gorgeous, but you're not my type and definitely *not* my age."

Jay seemed to simply bask in Levi's words and gave him a smug smile. "You just said I'm gorgeous. I can work with that."

"Why don't you just give up and admit you're into him?" Cody asked.

"Hmm, what a novel concept." Kennedy cocked his head and shot Cody a pointed look.

"Okay, okay. I think this shindig needs to be winding down." Micah threw his hands up. "Cole, let's go home. We can all use this week to talk to the community and gather members willing to speak on

Cole's behalf. If the board leaves it up to a town vote, we want to have as many people voting for Cole as possible."

"And, if I know Uncle Ed, he'll be working his little black heart out trying to get a very vocal part of the town on his side," Levi muttered.

"Okay, let's all work the town this week and keep in touch. We should be able to fill that meeting room with students and parents and community members all willing to stand and be heard." Cody headed toward the door.

"Or, to at least stand and been seen as one of Cole's supporters." Kennedy agreed.

"Do you think we've got enough people?" I bit at my thumb nail two weeks and many group meetings later.

"We definitely talked to enough people who were on your side, Cole. Guess it's going to depend on who shows up at the meeting." Cody shrugged as the six of us walked to the door of the building where my fate was to be decided.

"No matter what happens, you're great teacher and we've got your back." Micah pulled me close to his side. My first instinct was to pull away in case board members or townspeople would see, but his embrace was warm and safe, so I stayed a little longer. "You know I'll pack up and move with you in a heartbeat."

I smiled. "I know you would and I appreciate that more than you know, but I don't want to leave this place." Standing tall as I approached the meeting room door, I turned to face all of my friends. "I hope like hell this works out in my favor. Thank you all for your support."

"You got this," Jay whispered as he hugged me close.

When I opened the door, I first thought we were in the wrong room. At least two hundred people were packed inside the place.

"Holy shit!" Levi exclaimed.

Noticing at least forty of the people in the room were students from school, I quickly realized we were in the right place. And then I panicked. "It's not even going to be a fair fight." Heart sinking, my words trembled as my stomach began to churn.

"Damn straight it's not." Cody agreed.

"I can't go against all of these people." I was frozen in place.

"What are you talking about? All of these people are here for *you*." Micah pressed a gentle hand to the small of my back.

I forced myself to take in my surroundings. From the back of the room, I noted the large majority of those in attendance were congregated to my left. To my right, I saw Ed Edwards and about ten other people.

"They're here for me?" Tears stung my eyes. My thoughts returned to a school board meeting of the past when not even my parents had shown support for me.

"That's what being part of a community means. People stand up for you, they have your back, and they fight for you." Kennedy laid a hand on my shoulder. He threw his thumb over his shoulder. "Look at how many officers showed up. They aren't getting paid extra to be here. Sure, it's for crowd control if needed, but it's also to silently show support."

A voice from the front boomed, 'If everyone could settle in and find a seat, we'd like to get this proceeding started." The board president sat at a long table that spanned across the entire front of the room. Other board members filled the chairs to his right and left.

We took seats near the back of the room as those were all that remained. Glancing over toward Ed Edwards, I shivered slightly at the evil sneer on his face.

"Ignore him." Micah's whisper drew my attention. "Don't even look at him."

"This meeting is called to order." With those words from the board president, the meeting began, and I felt my entire future handed over to the folks of Blueridge Junction.

CHAPTER 19

MICAH

My heart soared when I saw the way so many BJ community members showed up to support Cole. In turn, they were supporting Cody, Levi, Jay, and myself and it felt damn good. It felt even better to show my dad that so many people were on our side and not his. I wished there didn't have to be sides, but Ed drew the line.

"Does anyone else feel like we're in that scene from Footloose? The one where the town is debating whether to allow dancing again?" Jay leaned over and whispered to our row.

Levi rolled his eyes but I caught the smile on his face before he clamped it down.

"Thank you all for being here." The president began. "We have quite the packed house, seems like maybe some people are pretty passionate. I think the last time a board meeting had this many people was when we voted on whether or not to allow soda in the school vending machines."

Chuckles filled the room.

"We'll start with a statement followed by Mr. Sutton. Then we will allow those who came to speak a chance to let their voice be heard. If Mr. Pierce would like to speak on his behalf, that will be allowed, as well. The board will vote. In the event of a tie, those in attendance will cast the final vote." The president nodded to the vice president who gave an imperceptible nod.

The younger woman locked her jaw, took a deep breath, and then began to read the statement from a piece of paper. "Mr. Cole Pierce is a social studies teacher at Blueridge Junction High School. Several concerned parents and community members contacted the board and Mr. Sutton, the principal, regarding Mr. Pierce's moral and character around impressionable students. The board placed Mr. Pierce on paid leave until the time a meeting could be held to discuss his employment. Please note, no accusations criminal or immoral have been made against Mr. Pierce, simply Blueridge Junction community members sharing their concerns." When she finished, the vice president looked almost as disgusted as I felt.

"Thank you." The president made a mark on the note pad in front of him. "Now, Mr. Sutton, you may come to the podium."

Mr. Sutton puffed up his chest and took his place behind the microphone. "Mr. Pierce teaches social studies at my school. His evaluations and performance have consistently been 'efficient' and 'highly efficient.'" With that, Mr. Sutton left the podium and returned to his seat.

"What the hell? That's all he's got to say?" Cody mumbled.

"Better short and sweet good positives than long drawn out negatives," Cole whispered and I could feel the nerves coming from him in waves.

"Thank you, Mr. Sutton." The board president consulted his notes. "Now, with that, we will open the microphone for any community members who would like to speak."

Dad was the first to bolt out of his seat and take to the stage. At least thirty others followed him and formed a line to wait their turn.

"You all know me. My family's been in Blueridge Junction since the very beginning. We've seen this town through thick and thin. I have a responsibility as a community member, business owner, parent, and friend to assure the mental, physical, and emotional well-being of all people, young and old, in BJ." My dad was laying the good ol' boy charm on thick. I prayed that none of the board members were buying his bullshit. "I ain't got nothin' against faggots. Live and let live I say. But I don't feel that lifestyle should be around our children. In my humble opinion, Mr. Pierce should not be allowed to teach in Blueridge Junction." Dad nodded toward the board and sat down.

Immediately upon the start of the next person's speech, I realized my dad's mistake. In his hurry to get to the stage so quickly, he hadn't anticipated that he'd be the only one speaking against Cole. I eyed the line of people. Not a single person was one I thought would have anything bad to say. Plus, Levi, Cody, and Kennedy were the last in line so I knew they'd finish things strong.

"You sure you don't want to speak?" I turned to Jay.

"I want to, but I worry my job and appearance would only hurt. People think I'm pretty and they like to watch me dance, they don't look at me as a fine upstanding citizen." Jay smiled sadly.

"You're more than a pretty face and great dancer," Cole whispered as he laid a comforting hand on Jay's leg. "I understand your hesitation, but if you change your mind, I'd be honored to have you speak for me."

Fellow teachers, business owners, housewives, railroad workers, and several students all took their turn to speak on Cole's behalf. None were professional speakers, but each and every one of the people hit on many of the same points. Cole's good-natured and friendly personality, his willingness to pitch in and help out, his exuberance for teaching and being a good role model for his students. Student after student spoke about how Cole helped them with a tough project, showed them how interesting social studies could actually be, encouraged them to reconsider college, and supported them while they worked to pull their grades up.

Sadie was the last student to take to the podium. "Mr. Pierce is as much a part of this town as any of us are. He fits in, he's one of us. Not only is he a great teacher, he's a good person, and I'm glad he's here. Mr. Pierce should definitely be allowed to continue teaching." She started to end her speech, but stopped and addressed the board. "Also, I've been studying up on laws, and I wanted to point out that it's already been made clear that Mr. Pierce has received nothing but good evaluations for his performance at school. There's been no accusations or charges made against him. At this point, to remove him from his job would look very much like discrimination. And any 'infraction' that may be marked against him in the coming weeks or months would scream bogus and make any lawyer giddy." Sadie ended her litany with a sweet smile and a toss of her hair. "I'm just saying." She shrugged and returned to her seat.

The board president pursed his lips and stared after her. "Duly noted," his words sounded anything but pleased, but the vice president was smiling like she'd just won the lottery.

Levi's words were straight to the point. "I'm gay. You all have known that since I was in junior high. I'd hate to lose my job because of that. Would you want to lose your job because you're overweight? Would your weight rub off on kids? What if you have tattoos? Should you lose your job because you may taint a child with your ink? Maybe Ed's Autos should be shut down for having a gay mechanic." Levi shrugged. "I'm just sayin', Cole's a good teacher and has done nothing wrong but be who he is. Nothing he's done is hurting students. Taking him away from his teaching position *would* hurt students." With that, Levi left the stage.

Cody stood and just stared at the board members and then at the crowd. "You know, it's funny to me how many of you have no problem casting stones towards others but want your own kinks and fetishes kept out of it." He paused to let that sink in. "Pretty much everyone in this town knows why I close the restaurant on Sundays. Many of you know because you've come to participate or watch. If no one is bothering you, why bother Cole?"

Jay stood suddenly and interrupted Cody. "Sorry, I wasn't going to speak. But, in the same vein as what Cody's saying, I know about the things many of you do and say when you're drinking. Should watching dancers and paying for lap dances get you ousted from your job? Because, if so, I've got quite the list I could start naming." Jay just smiled and sat down quickly.

Kennedy was the last to take the stand. "No laws have been broken by Cole Pierce. End of story." He looked straight at my dad. "However, several laws have been broken by someone attempting to get Cole to leave town. When that didn't work, this pathetic tactic was used. If anyone needs to be voted out, it's sure not Cole."

"Mr. Pierce, would you care to speak on your behalf?" The board president appeared to be aggravated with the number of speakers and the time the meeting was taking.

Cole nodded and stood.

I love you, I love you, I love you I repeated over and over in hopes of bolstering him as he walked to the front. No matter how the meeting turned out, I was so damned proud of him.

When he reached the stage, Cole held onto the podium as if clinging to a lifesaver. "Thank you so very much to all of you who came out tonight to show your support. It means the world to me." Pausing, he cleared his throat. "I won't take too much of your time. Plain and simple, I love Blueridge Junction. I love the people, I love the beauty, and I love the sense of community. I've even started getting fond of how everyone knows your business. Hell, I've found myself enjoying the rumble of the trains as they pass through and when they are switching tracks."

A murmur of approval skittered through the room.

"I am a good teacher. I'm a good person. I'd like to stay and make a career out of teaching and make a home here in BJ." He shrugged. "That's pretty much all it comes down to. Thanks."

Before Cole had even returned to his seat, the president was speaking. "Okay, we've come to the point of the meeting where the board members will cast their votes. In the unlikely event of a tie," the man was entirely too sure of his board members' votes in my opinion, "those residents who are of legal voting age and present will be allowed to vote. We'll go down the line. Please state *YES* if you feel Mr. Pierce should stay on at Blueridge Junction High School, say *NO* if you think he should step down."

"Yes."

"Yes."

"No."

"No."

"Yes."

The final vote came to the president. "No."

A gasp went through the crowd.

"Quiet down," the man boomed. "Let's make this quick. No one under age eighteen can vote."

When the crowd of students protested, the president continued. "That's not a new rule. Sorry. Only those of legal voting age." The president looked to the crowd. "If you choose not to vote, that is your decision. Now, let's have the *YES* votes to my right and the *NO* votes to my left."

Cole was not allowed to vote. None of the uniformed officers could vote because they were there as town employees at the time even if they weren't getting paid. With very few of the students old enough to vote and a disappointing number of people who chose not to vote, my stomach began to flutter in anticipation. Would we have enough?

When the non-voters had been moved to the back and the sides clearly taken, the vote was once again a tie. My heart sank.

"Is there anyone else who would like to cast their vote?" The vice president spoke up.

My heart ached. I wanted to hold Cole in my arms. I hated the fact he looked so alone as he watched his fate play out.

In a split second, I heard the collective gasp of the room and saw the evil smile on my dad's face as the door opened.

My mom.

"Mrs. Edwards, have you come to vote?" The president asked and smirked as if he knew the answer and the outcome.

Cody's mom, Marian, stepped from a row on the *YES* side and took my mom's hand. Marian leaned in and whispered something to her and my mom nodded through tears.

Dad stood up and pointed threateningly at Mom "Yeah, she wants to vote. And she knows how to vote if she's knows what the fuck is good for her."

Mom looked directly at me. "Are you happy? Does Cole make you happy?"

Forcing back the anger at my dad and unsureness at my mom's arrival, I could only nod.

"Woman!" Dad roared.

She turned to look at my dad. Returning her gaze to me, she sniffled. "I'm sorry, Micah."

My heart sank. "Mom, please…"

"No, let me finish." Mom wiped tears from her eyes. "I'm sorry I made you live with him, I'm sorry I wasn't strong enough." She turned and smiled at Marian. "But, I want to fix that, I want to be strong enough now."

"Whatever you need, we're here," Marian replied.

With downcast eyes, my mom took her place on the *YES* side of the room.

The entire place erupted in cheers. Amidst the happy chaos, I saw my dad storm from the room, but my only thought was to get to Cole.

When I reached him, Cole had sat down on a chair and had his head in his hands.

"Baby, what's wrong? This is good news!" I grabbed him by the hands and pulled him up to stand.

With a sniffle and a choked laugh, he hugged me. "I just didn't think it would turn out this way. I owe your mom big time."

"Let's go say hi." I guided him over to where the entire gang was standing with Cody's parents and my mom.

"Mom, thank you." I pulled her into a hug.

"I'm sorry it took me so long." Mom cried into my chest.

"Your mom is going to be staying with us." Marian spoke up and Hank nodded.

"Sounds good." I agreed. Knowing Mom would be away from Dad felt good.

"Ms. Edwards, you let me know if Ed gives you any trouble." Kennedy interjected. "In fact, you let any single officer in this town knows if Ed so much as breathes your way. We'll take care of it."

When the crowd broke up, the six of us headed outside.

"Well, Cole, it looks like you're officially a BJ Boy." Levi slapped him on the back.

Cole laughed and pressed himself against my side as we walked toward the parking lot. "Thanks. I'll wear the title with pride."

"I want to be a BJ Boy." Jay pouted.

"You don't just get to *be* a BJ Boy." Levi shook his head at Jay as we reached our vehicles.

"Yeah, you have to fight for it." I pressed Cole against the side of my truck and kissed him until we were both struggling to breathe. "I love you, baby. Welcome to BJ."

"Thank you for fixing me." Cole murmured against my mouth.

"What are you talking about? There was *nothing* wrong with you." I pulled back to look at him closely.

"You once told me that you like to take things apart, fix them, and rebuild them. That's what you did for me. You broke me down and rebuilt a better me. A stronger more courageous me. There was nothing *wrong* with me before, but you helped me see I didn't have to hide. I love you for that." Cole's tears slid down his chin.

"And we can spend the rest of our lives making each other the best we can be."

Placing a soft kiss to Cole's lips, we climbed into the truck and headed up Blueridge Hill to begin living the rest of our lives.

Epilogue

Cole

"What time is dinner?" Micah called from the shower as I dressed in the bedroom. We were staying on in Levi's guest house while our new home on Blueridge Hill was being built.

"Sadie, your mom, and Marian are shopping for Sadie's graduation dress and some college supplies. We are supposed to meet everyone at BJ's at six-thirty." I popped my head into the bathroom and smiled when Micah's eye caught mine.

"Mmmm, so we have some time to kill before we leave." Micah slid the shower door open and waggled his brows at me. "Whatever shall we do with that time, Professor?"

"I don't know. What do you think, Papi?" I joked.

"You know, those nicknames are ridiculous when Jay uses them, but somehow they work.

However when we use them, we just sound like idiots." Micah laughed.

"So true." I returned to the bedroom and came back with two ties. "Which of these do you think I should wear to graduation next weekend?"

"I love them both. You wear one and I'll wear the other." Micah climbed from the shower and wrapped himself in a towel. "Better yet, how about I use them right now and tie you to the bed and have my wicked way with you?" Micah crowded against me until I ran into the sink.

Lifting myself up, I sat on the counter and spread my legs to let him step closer. Wrapping my arms around his hot, damp shoulders, I kissed his neck and trailed my tongue through water droplets by his ear until I reached his mouth. "Careful, Cody's and Kennedy's kinks may be rubbing off on you."

We laughed, but Micah sobered quickly. "You like going to the restaurant some Sundays, right? I mean, we don't *have* to go if you don't enjoy it."

"Are you kidding? I love it. Who knew there were so many kinky fuckers in town?" I ran my short nails down Micah's back and bit my lip when his body shivered at the sensation.

"Well, a lot of the people who come to Sundays aren't actually from BJ." Micah grabbed my hips and yanked me forward until our dicks touched. "There's way too much fabric between us." He took my head in his hands and tipped my mouth up to his kiss. "Does kinky bother you?"

"Hell no," I mumbled against his lips.

A shrill tone vibrated the sink to my left and we both groaned.

"Damn." Micah pulled away just far enough to grab the phone. "It's Mitch."

"You better take it." I trailed a finger down his arm until I reached his hand. Taking it in mine, I gave a gentle squeeze.

Things between Micah and his mom had gotten better the past few months. Things between Micah and Ed had gotten...well, worse wasn't the word. Ed had left town after I was allowed back to teaching. Mitch had called to tell us Ed was with him and not doing well. Over the past couple months, Mitch would call with brief updates on Ed, but they were mostly the same. Ed was drinking heavily. Ed was angry. Ed was making threats. *"Micah, I don't trust him back in BJ, but having here is driving me crazy. He's not in his right mind, man."*

Micah gave my hand a return squeeze and accepted the call. "Mitch, you're on speaker with Cole and me. What's up?"

"Can you meet me somewhere? We need to talk." Mitch's voice sounded tired.

"Where are you?"

"Just a couple miles outside of BJ. Can you be at the house?"

Micah's gaze met mine and we both shrugged. "Yeah. Fifteen minutes?"

Mitch agreed and hung up.

"What do you think he needs? Do you think Ed is with him?" I worried my lip.

"Nah, I don't think Mitch would bring Dad back around Mom." Micah stripped his towel to pull on his clothes. "But, I'm going to give Kennedy a heads up just in case."

Micah called Kennedy to fill him in on the little we knew while I grabbed my shoes. In a few minutes, we were headed to Micah's childhood home.

Settling ourselves on the front porch, we watched as Kennedy's police car pulled up the drive and Mitch's sleek Corvette arrived a few moments later. Kennedy stayed in his car and texted Micah, "I'm here if needed."

Mitch climbed from his car and stretched. Climbing the stairs, he offered a small wave toward his brother and I. Mitch and I had spoken a few times on the phone, but never met in person. He was shorter and broader than Micah, but many of their features were the same.

Mitch lowered himself to one of the porch chairs. "How can I love a place and miss it just as much as I hate it and want to stay away?" He mused as he glanced around the property.

"What's up? Where's Dad?" Micah skipped his brother's ponderings and jumped straight in.

"Dad is dead."

Mitch's words seemed a mixture of exhaustion and relief. I heard no sorrow or mourning in them.

"What?" Micah sounded shocked, but not upset.

"Drank himself into a stupor and never woke up. Coroner says alcohol poisoning. Liver just shut down. He'd been killing himself with liquor for a while." Mitch shook his head. "Sorry it took so long for me to get here. He died a week ago. I probably should have called, but I got busy with the medical stuff and the cremation and the legal stuff."

Perfect example of the no love loss relationship between Mitch and Micah.

"I'm sorry you were stuck dealing with all of that." Micah spoke as if he just felt the need to say words.

"No problem. The man was an ass to me and even worse to you. No reason for you to have to leave BJ to deal with it all...or mom." Mitch stared down the driveway. "But, there's a real reason I came here. I could have told you all of that on the phone."

Micah tensed beside me.

"Dad left Ed's Autos to me." Mitch pulled an envelope from his pocket and tapped it against his hand.

"Yeah, I figured as much." Micah's words held hurt, but no surprise.

"Well, you likely didn't figure it all." Mitch opened the envelope. "I don't want the damn shop. Never have, never will."

Micah raised his brow in question. "Why'd you let Dad think you wanted it?"

"Kept me on his good side for the most part." Mitch pulled a stack of papers from the envelope. "After he died, I talked to a lawyer. I've signed the business over to you. I'm sure there's a few more legal things we'll have to deal with in the upcoming months, but the shop is yours to do with as you see fit. Close it, change it, burn it to the ground for all I care."

Micah was quiet for a long moment while he read the papers Mitch handed to him.

"Thank you. I know it's never meant a lot to you, but the shop means a lot to me." Micah reached for and squeezed Cole's hand. "I want to make it bigger and better. I want to run it with respect, honesty, and integrity instead of fear and threats like Dad."

"Go for it, man. You always did have a knack for the mechanics side and the business side. I wish you the best of luck." Mitch stood.

"That's it? You're leaving?" Micah followed Mitch to the steps.

"I may try to meet up with Mom, but yeah, I've had all the BJ I can take for one day." Mitch headed to his car.

"Hey, you've always got a place here if you need it." Micah called out.

"Thanks. I appreciate it. Don't expect me to come back and work for you, but it's nice to know the offer is there." Mitch smirked as he opened the door.

"Keep in touch?" Micah and I had reached the 'Vette.

"Yeah." Mitch fired the engine up. "Oh, one more thing. Dad spent most of his time drunk and mumbling about how he was going to come back to BJ and 'run that faggot off once and for all.' I'm not sure if that means anything to you, but I thought you should know."

We stood and watched Mitch drive away.

Kennedy pulled up beside us. "I'll give you guys a moment. See you at dinner."

When we were alone, I wrapped Micah in my arms. "You okay?"

He nodded. "Yeah. It's weird. I feel like I should be upset over my dad dying, but I only feel relief that he's not going to be around to hurt you or my mom or me."

"So, you're a business owner now, huh?" I knew Micah would process his dad's death in his own time and I'd be there to talk with him and listen when he was ready.

Micah smiled down at me. "I'm a business owner. The shop is *mine.*"

"You already have plans?" I asked even though I knew the answer.

"Hell yeah. The first thing to change is the name. I'll have to work on it, but I don't want my dad's name tainting it any longer." Micah was all but skipping as we walked to his truck to go back to the guest house.

"Want to go see the progress on the house?" I pointed toward the lane that would go to our new home site.

Micah took the turn. "Even better idea. The workers will be done for today. I say we christen some rooms."

"We are supposed to go to dinner." I offered a slight protest, but didn't put up too much of a fight.

"We can be late." Micah grabbed my hand and pulled me close to him on the truck seat.

And we were. Very late.

From the Author

Don't miss my other male/male romance books in the <u>Something About Him</u> series!

<u>author.to/ADEllisAmazon</u>

THANK YOU FOR READING! I hope you enjoyed; please take a moment to leave a review. If you're reading on a file/device that doesn't take you to a review option, please consider finding the book on the platform of your choice and giving a star rating and a short review. It doesn't have to be long and drawn out, just a few sentences about how it made you feel, what you liked/didn't like. THANK YOU!!

If you are interested in my male/female contemporary romance series (Torey Hope) or my other male/male romance books, please check out my <u>website</u> to find information about all of my books. Or, search your favorite book platform for my name and see if something tickles your fancy.

A.D. Ellis

ABOUT THE AUTHOR

A.D. Ellis is an Indiana girl, born and raised. She spends much of her time in central Indiana teaching alternative education in the inner city of Indianapolis, being a mom to two amazing school-aged children, and laughing at a precocious cat. A lot of her time is also devoted to phone call avoidance and her hatred of cooking.

She loves chocolate, wine, pizza, and naps along with reading and writing romance. These loves don't leave much time for housework, much to the chagrin of her husband of nearly two decades. Who would pick cleaning the house over a nap or a good book? She uses any extra time to increase her fluency in sarcasm.

FREE books-- sign up at bit.ly/ADEllisNews for a FREE male/female romance. Sign up at http://www.subscribepage.com/ADEllisNewsMMR omance for a FREE male/male romance book.

Facebook www.facebook.com/adellisauthor

Twitter www.twitter.com/ADEllisAuthor

Website http://adellisauthor.com/

ACKNOWLEDGEMENTS

This is always one of the hardest parts of finishing a book, but quite possibly the most important part! It's so hard because I fear I'll miss someone who has helped me out, supported me, been a listening ear, or offered advice and encouragement. If I miss listing your name here, please know it wasn't on purpose, and I love you dearly!

A dear friend once again made this book possible. I'm not sure he understands how much his input means to me and how he shapes my stories with his words, answers, experiences, and heart. Thank you, Brett, as always. Don't ever doubt your potential and how lucky people are to know you.

And, to Gage. You are truly an amazing person. Thank you, again, for all of your help and input. Not to get all mushy, but you have an incredible future ahead of you because you can do absolutely anything you set your mind to. I feel blessed to get to watch you reach the stars.

To David, Donny, Kurt, and Chris- while your input on this book was sparse, you've already helped me so much with the following stories that I would be remiss if I didn't mention you here.

To my friend, fellow author, and cover designer, Kay Simone at <u>Kay Simone Creative</u>. Thank you for listening to my vision and making it beautiful! You are a superb talent and I'm lucky to call you my designer.

To my dear beta readers. Your input, feedback, and encouragement has proven invaluable to me! I truly trust you all and value your opinions more than you'll probably ever understand. Thank you to my newest betas as well. When I needed fresh new eyes who had never read any of these characters you were there for me and helped me so much!

To my Ellis Elite Private Discussion Group— THANK YOU! Those of you who list me in contests and comments and shout outs all the time, you're amazing and I love you for always working to get my name out there! If I start naming people here, I'll be sure to miss some; just know if you've ever shared my name or my books, it means the world to me and I appreciate you more than you'll ever know!

To my READERS!! You are what keeps me going. You are the reason I write some days. When I don't feel like I have it in me, I'll get a message or comment from a reader about how a story of mine has touched them, and *that* will be the inspiration and motivation for me to write. As long as these stories are in my head, I'll keep sharing them with you.

To the BLOGGERS who read and review and share my books!! You are beyond a shadow of a doubt some of the most dedicated and selfless people I've ever known! Thank you so much for being such a support to those of us who have stories to tell. I love BLOGGERS!

To my Juice Box ladies! Thank you so much for welcoming me into your crew and sharing your knowledge, experience, advice, and fun with me! Having some real-life authors/friends I can collaborate with is a great feeling. Dance parties, lunches, movies, videos, wine, painting, pizza, sushi, cookies…the list goes on and on! Thank you for letting me be a Juice Boxer!

Ann-Katrin Byrde, thank you for polishing my blurb and making it shine!

To my fellow authors. Those of you who read my work, share your work with me, cross-promote with me, and offer advice and support, THANK YOU! You make this a little easier and enjoyable.

To my family and friends. I know most of you don't understand my obsession with getting these stories out of my head and on paper, but you're proud of me either way. Some of you get to read my books, some of you get to see cover ideas, some of you have to watch me lose myself in a story, some of you have to hear me vent about the hard parts of all of this; all of you love me and support me and for that, I am truly lucky and grateful.

CONNECT WITH A.D. ELLIS

Follow my website

http://www.adellisauthor.com or find me on Facebook

http://www.facebook.com/adellisauthor

If you want updates about releases, interviews, sales, giveaways, and more please sign up for my newsletter bit.ly/ADEllisNews

You can also find me on Twitter http://www.twitter.com/ADEllisAuthor

Find me on Spotify if you'd like to listen to my playlists (mainly the songs I listened to while writing). Just search for A.D. Ellis.